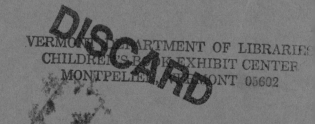

Get on out of here,
Philip Hall

Get on out of here, Philip Hall

by BETTE GREENE

The Dial Press : New York

Published by
The Dial Press
1 Dag Hammarskjold Plaza
New York, New York 10017

Library of Congress Cataloging in Publication Data
Greene, Bette, 1934–   Get on out of here, Philip Hall
Summary: While trying to outdo Philip Hall, Beth
learns an important but painful lesson about leadership.
[1. Leadership—Fiction. 2. Friendship—Fiction] I. Title.
PZ7.G8283Ge   [Fic]   80–22775
ISBN 0–8037–2871–9   AACR 1
ISBN 0–8037–2872–7 (lib. bdg.)

Contents

Get on out of here,
Philip Hall

Chapter 1

Get on out of here, Philip Hall

"And to all you members of the Old Rugged Cross Church," I said, looking at my reflection in my dressing-table mirror, "I sure do want to thank you all for giving me this here Abner Jerome Brady Leadership Award."

When my warm moist breath began to fog the mirror, I moved back a ways. "Why, I wasn't any more expecting this honor than the man in the moon, 'cause I've almost forgotten that it's been almost a year since I caught those thieving turkey rustlers. And I reckon that there ain't hardly nobody alive that doesn't know that I, Elizabeth Lorraine Lambert, is the number-one best student in Miss Johnson's class.

"Course, I guess most of you will remember that for three consecutive years, I've been president and chief presiding officer of the Pretty Pennies Girls Club of Pocahontas, Arkansas. But just because I've accomplished all these things doesn't mean that I'm the only one worthy of your fine award. No, sir! Why, I reckon that there are just plenty of folks (even including some boys!) who deserve this honor every bit as much as me."

Pausing long enough to allow the full extent of my humbleness to be absorbed by my imaginary audience, I brought my face close to the mirror and caught my mother's reflection. I whirled quickly to face her. "Now, Ma, I know you're anxious to hear my speech, but you're just going to have to wait until six o'clock tonight like everybody else."

She didn't say anything, but she looked troubled. Did she forget all about the three-hundred-dollar scholarship money that comes right along with the Brady Award? And did Ma also forget that before I become Randolph County's first veterinarian, I'm going to need all the scholarship money I can get? Just before seating herself on my bed, she smoothed out a slight wrinkle in my chenille spread. "Beth, honey, I don't rightly know how to say this to you. . . ."

"Grandma ain't ailing, is she? I mean she's still coming to hear my speech this evening?"

She nodded. "Mr. Preston Simpson, who works at the Walnut Ridge Gulf Station, is going to drop your• grandma off right in front of the church grounds."

"If Grandma is coming, then there can't be much of nothing wrong," I concluded, trying to jolly Ma up by giving her a tickle under her chin.

"Maybe something is wrong," my mother said. "Maybe it ain't. Don't rightly know. Now, I sure don't want to be disturbing you, what with the ceremony not much more'n two hours away. But I do, truth to tell, feel a little . . . a little unsettled about your speech."

"About my speech? Didn't I tell every member of this family that I didn't want nobody—not even Baby Benjamin—listening to me practice my speech? Well? What about my speech?" I asked, afraid I might hear something that wasn't complimentary.

Ma sighed as though she was getting ready to do heavy work. "Winning the Abner Brady Award is some honor. Yes, sir, it sure is some fine honor—"

"But—" I said to let her know I realized there was more coming.

"But," she repeated, "you just all the time going around counting your Bradys before they hatch. And ain't you a little too busy puffing yourself up? Tooting your own horn?"

"Who me?!" I asked, striking my chest with my index finger.

"How many other folks you got hidden around this room, girl?"

"Oh, Ma . . ."

I heard my mother sigh, as though it was now time to get down to serious business. "Beth, if you is half as great as you got yourself believing that you are, then you don't have to talk about it in your speech. No, sir! All you really have to do is give folks a little time and they'll up and discover it all by themselves."

At five o'clock Ma, Pa, Baby Benjamin, and I got into the cab of our pickup. Must be some special evening, sure enough. Usually my older sister, Annie, sat up front. But tonight Fancy Annie was sitting out back with my brother Luther, dangling her feet from the tailgate just like any ordinary person.

Where our dirt road leads onto the highway, Pa brought his truck to a momentary stop before turning to face me. "Little Beth, little Beth, why I couldn't be any more proud of you if you was twins. Being chosen the best young leader in our church. My, my, my, now ain't that some something!"

"Oh, I is so happy that you is happy, Pa," I told him. "But want to know something? Not everybody is all that happy for me."

This time his smile showed off a set of teeth as white

as blackboard chalk. "Reckon I don't need a hundred guesses when one will do. You is speaking of Phil Hall?"

I nodded. "The very same Philip Hall who's going around acting like he ain't got no time for nobody in this here world but Ginny—Ginny-the-gorgeous. But everybody knows that she ain't got the sense that God gave to a single one of Luther's precious pigs! So how could— Well, what does he like about Ginny?"

Pa began laughing so hard that Ma had to come right out and tell him to keep his mind on his driving. "I think," he said finally, "that you is still sweet on that boy."

"Oh, no sir, I ain't," I told him. "Why, I don't pay that boy no more mind than a speck of dust blowing in the wind. Why, on this very morning Philip Hall told me that I shouldn't be so sure of winning something that I ain't already won."

Pa squeezed out another chuckle or two. "Everybody knows what's bothering him. For better than a year now, you've been stealing all his thunder and all his glory. There ain't hardly none left for nobody else."

"You can sure say that again," said Ma, sounding more resigned than joyous.

"Remember last month?" asked Pa. "At the Old Rugged Cross Church picnic when everybody was searching beneath the river for that boy? Heard the Reverend Ross himself say nobody could be that long underwater and live. Exact words he said was 'Only the good right arm of

7

the Lord could save poor Phil Hall now.' Well, he no sooner got them words out of his mouth than you came riding through the picnic grounds on a borrowed tractor with a hurt Phil. Lordy!"

Ma must have clearly seen the sight in her own mind because a laugh as deep as a peal of thunder started up in her. "Phil Hall ain't altogether wrong when he tells you not to go counting what you ain't already won, and yet . . ." She had to stop talking until she got a hold on her laughter. "I don't think I'll ever forget, not if I live to be a hundred, the look on his face when your own calf, Madeline, and not his fancy Hall's Dairy Farm calf, Leonard, won first prize at the county fair.—Well, what did you tell that young rascal when he told you not to go thinking you won what you haven't as yet won?"

"Well," I said. "First thing I did was stare him straight in the eye. Second thing I did was spit out the corner of my mouth, and the last thing I did was to say, 'Get yourself on out of here, Philip Hall!' "

In a meadow directly behind the Old Rugged Cross Church was Roscoe Barnes's sunshine-yellow tent. The flags flying on top called attention to the fearless Mr. Barnes and his death-defying animal acts, but our church members insist that the most death-defying thing Mr. Barnes ever in his life did was to try to sneak out of town in the middle of the night without paying our church for the use of its land.

8

Anyway, Mr. Barnes made off with his truck, his lions, his tigers, and his life, but not with his tent. No, sir, not with his tent! During the heat of the summer, it's been real nice hearing our sermons from the somewhat cooler insides of a circus tent. And on a breezy September night like tonight, nothing could be more perfect.

After parking our truck on the grassy edge of the highway, we made our way with the rest of the folks through patches of purple wild flowers toward the tent.

"Beth! Hey!" I whirled around to see Esther running up from behind. "Guess who I saw? You'll never in a million years guess who I saw!"

"Philip Hall?"

"Don't take no million years to guess him," she said.

"Well, why don't you just tell me?"

"Who I saw was none other than Miss Ramona Thomas!"

"Really?"

"Really and truly."

"Does she want to take my picture now?" I asked.

Ma touched my arm. "Hold on to a little modesty, Beth honey. You ain't saved the world yet. And when Miss Ramona is ready to take your picture, she won't have no bit of trouble finding you. And that's for sure!"

"Oh, you is going to be famous!" shrieked Esther. "Going to have your photograph spread all across *The Pocahontas Weekly News*."

Just then I spotted Philip Hall outside the tent wearing a brand-new tan suit. That was kind of amazing, considering it was only this year the pants on his old blue suit had begun to ride high on his leg. As he stared up at our church's slightly peeling steeple, I noticed once again how tall he stood. Just like one of the king's own soldiers, only better-looking—a whole lot better-looking.

"Howdy do, Philip," I said, smiling enough to prove to him that I don't care beans if he likes Ginny-the-not-so very-gorgeous.

I watched his body stiffen as though he was fixing to run—or fight. Then he sighed. "Hi, Beth. Know something?"

"No," I answered.

"Remember what I said about not counting your Abner Brady Awards before you win?"

"Oh, that."

"Yeah, well." He began to examine the middle button on his left sleeve with all the interest of somebody who had never before in his life seen a button. "I guess maybe you can count them. If you want to."

"I can?"

"Sure, I mean well . . . well, why not? 'Cause I reckon I've come to believe what I didn't even want to think about."

"And what is that, Philip?"

He smiled as though the joke was on him. "About you being the only real natural-born leader."

"Oh, you is doing real fine, Philip," I said, smiling back at him and pumping his hand up and down. " 'Cause admitting the truth is mighty good for you. It's the grown-up thing to do."

Just then our Bible teacher, Miss Bernice, called all us junior members of the Old Rugged Cross Church into a huddle behind the tent. "Now, nobody's got no reason to feel scared," she said, making me feel, for the first time, scared. " 'Cause I know you'll all do exactly what you were taught. So when the fiddler commences playing 'Onward, Christian Soldiers,' just throw your heads back and march on in."

Jordan Jones, who comprises exactly fifty percent of the Jones twins, had all ten fingers crossed tight enough to stop circulation. Don't go telling me that he, of all people, thinks he got a chance at the Abner Brady? Why Jordan Jones is so lacking in leadership that not even his mangy old dog, Buster, bothers to obey his commands. Come to think of it, the only person in this world who possesses less leadership ability than Jordan Jones is his identical twin, Joshua.

Personally, I think it's wonderful that the Old Rugged Cross Church would give the Abner Brady Award to the one student showing the best leadership, but it's probably not what you'd call fair to Philip Hall, Jordan, Joshua, and all the others. I mean when you think how disappointing and embarrassing it must be for them.

Having to sit there on that platform, waiting for the preacher to announce an award that they can never even hope to receive.

I heard the fiddler begin tuning up and then Miss Bernice lightly touched her lips to signal for quiet. That's when all twenty of us got ready to take that long, solitary walk all the way up to the front of the packed tent.

The musician struck up the tune, but it was my memory that supplied the words:

> *Onward, Christian soldiers,*
> *Marching as to war,*
> *With the cross of Jesus*
> *Going on before!* ...

Miss Bernice gave Zoey Abbott the nod to begin moving. Then, counting under her breath, our teacher signaled Bonnie Blake to follow. Next was Ginny (the gorgeous) Campbell, but I didn't watch her. I sneaked a look at Philip Hall to see if he was watching her. He *was* watching her! Not that I care.

Following the gorgeous one were Bess Eaton and Danny Franklin. And then it was his turn. Philip Hall's. After him came the Jones boys—Jordan before Joshua. I was next. Suddenly it dawned on me that I was *next!*

My stomach felt as though it was being squeezed through the wringer of Ma's old washing machine. And what exactly was wrong with my feet? Lifting them was too heavy a burden. I wondered if I was coming down with a disease so terrible that not even doctors would dare give it a name. Either that or I was being sucked into a deep dark pit of quicksand.

With sudden and compelling force, I was shoved through the tent's opening. I felt myself moving, actually moving down the aisle. Faces, all the faces that I grew up knowing, stared at me as I made my way toward the raised stage. But it wasn't until I sat down on the metal chair next to Jordan—it could have been Joshua—that my breathing came back.

Finally Albert Lee Woods, our last classmate, took his seat and the fiddler stopped playing. Then the Reverend Ross, the best pastor the Old Rugged Cross Church ever had, strode up to the center of the stage. Looking out over the rows of faces, he announced in celestial tones, "Brothers and sisters . . . let us pray."

First he prayed for the sinners and then he prayed for the sick and eventually he even got around to praying for all us candidates for the highest honor that the Old Rugged Cross Church can bestow: the Abner Jerome Brady Leadership Award.

Well, to be perfectly truthful, I got to wishing that the good Reverend would make do with a mite less praying. Announcing Elizabeth Lorraine Lambert the winner, isn't that what everybody was really waiting for?

With his back toward us and his face toward the audience, the Reverend Ross lifted his arms, making the soft folds of his black robe look like great wings, fully strong enough to soar up to heaven's door. "Well, brothers and sisters of the congregation, I reckon I know what you've all been waiting for," said the preacher, just as though his mind had been taking orders from mine. "And I for one aim to get on with it. Ahem . . . ahem, but first I want to tell you a story from the Bible which will illustrate just the kind of leadership that we have been looking for.

"Has to do with little David and what it was he said to the King of the Israelites after slaying mighty Goliath. Little David bowed to the king and then he said, 'I am your servant.' " The preacher's voice grew louder. " 'I am YOUR servant!!!' And so little David not only saved his people from destruction, but he saved them with humbleness and humility. He used his leadership wisely. Not for himself, never for himself, but for the protection of the Hebrews and for the greater glory of God. Hallelujah!"

From all across the depth and breadth of the tent, voices called out, "Amen. Amen, brother!"

Then the Reverend Ross did what he always does on important occasions: He cleared his throat. "And so the person we've chosen is a top student at the J. T. Williams School. . . ."

When you is number-one best student, then there ain't better anybody can get, I thought.

"The person we've chosen," continued the Reverend Ross, "is also well known as a leader outside of the classroom, with important club activities."

Being president and chief presiding officer of the Pretty Pennies Girls Club of Pocahontas, Arkansas, for three straight years is showing leadership aplenty!

"And finally the person we have picked is well known and admired all around and about Pocahontas. . . ."

Nobody was better known or more admired in Pocahontas than me after I had captured those terrible turkey thieves with only a BB gun. *The Pocahontas Weekly News* wrote that my feat was a real heroic act. An act just packed to the fill with courage and daring.

The Reverend Ross pulled out a long, important-looking envelope from the blackness of his garments and gave it a slap. ". . . And the person chosen is not only going to get a fine trophy but this here scholarship money. Three hundred dollars worth of scholarship money!"

With what sounded like a single voice, the entire audience spoke: "OHhhh . . ."

Then our preacher called for Mrs. Rebecca Grant, president of the Old Rugged Cross Church Sisterhood, to bring the trophy. From the back of the tent, Mrs. Grant moved with uncommon dignity, carrying the gleaming silver cup in the center of a piece of purple material.

And again the entire tent seemed to speak with one voice: "AHHHhhh . . ."

Once more the Reverend Ross lifted those arms that looked like angel wings. "And so, folks, with no more dillying and no more dallying, I'm now going to ask the youngun that we all came here today to honor to please stand up."

This time I didn't need a forceful two-handed shove from Miss Bernice to come to my feet. I rose, standing straight and proud behind the Reverend Ross. But he just continued talking as though I wasn't already standing there.

"So now without no more further fanfare or ado, let's all give a big hand of applause to the recipient of the Abner Jerome Brady Leadership Award. Because our winner, like little David, knows exactly how to lead quietly and humbly. Would you kindly stand up, Philip Marvin Hall!"

Philip Hall? I stood there thinking that it sounded as though he said Philip Hall. Why would he say Philip Hall? Then with all the pain of a hundred wasp stings, I answered my own question. All at once I didn't know what to do. I didn't even know what to think.

I saw that all heads was turning toward me. Here and there I heard a giggle. Then the tent was alive, not just with giggles or laughter, but ridicule—who could they possibly find to ridicule? My God, they were ridiculing me!

Beyond row upon row of faces shaking with mocking laughter, I caught sight of one unmoving face. My mother's. My mother's face looking every bit as pained as that time she burned her hand on the cookstove.

Bolting from the stage, I knocked down my folding chair. The sound of metal striking metal shattered through the tent as I ran down the center aisle toward the opening. Have to run! Have to hide! A tunnel. A hole. Down deep, deep as an earthworm.

Faster than I had ever run before, I ran out of the tent and through the moonlit clearing. Ran on and on toward the dark and mysterious forest.

Even though the night was cool, I felt streams of sweat flowing down my forehead. Soon the back of my best dress was as wet as when I put it through the wringer of our washing machine.

The forest was closer now. There a person would be safe from mocking eyes and ridiculing laughter. But running was getting harder all the time. My heart knocked painfully against my rib cage. As I gasped for breath, for just a little more breath, I told myself I could not stop running: See, the forest line isn't so very far away now. Have to go on because I just have to find me someplace to hide. Hide in a place where nobody will ever again lay their eyes on the awful likes of Beth Lambert.

Half running, half stumbling, I reached out my arms and touched trees. At last I was entering the forest. A place where the twining and intertwining of branches shut out the nosy light of the moon. I dropped to my knees on the dark, damp earth before completely collapsing next to the trunk of an aged oak.

Never in my whole life had I ever been so alone in a place so dark. Not that I was afraid . . . but still, I had never before been alone in a place so dark.

When some of the fiercer, more persistent rays of early morning sun worked their way through the branches, I rubbed the sleep from my eyes, relieved that I had actually made it through the night.

I got to my feet before stretching. My neck felt stiff. Looking down, I recognized the thick root where I had rested my head through the long and frightening night.

I walked out of the forest, crossed the clearing, and started following Highway 67 toward home. Throughout the five-mile walk, I worked hard to keep from thinking about what had happened during the terrible night of the Abner Brady.

Instead I filled my head with thoughts about the Arkansas Highway Department and how they do a real nice, neat job of painting yellow stripes down the middle of the highway. When I didn't want to think anymore about highways, I thought about telephone poles and how pretty they'd look painted pink.

But after a while I wasn't thinking about yellow stripes or pink poles. I was too busy giving my full sympathetic attention to my sore neck and my broken spirit.

I turned off the highway just at that familiar spot where a faded black arrow pointed down a narrow dirt road.

1 mile

↑

Lambert Farm

good turkeys

good pigs

From the direction of my house I heard so much barking that I was certain every dog in Randolph County had come to the same party. When I came close, I saw some men holding on to their overexcited hound dogs by leather leashes. And in the field in front of our house there was enough cars and pickup trucks to fill up Speedy Russell's used-car lot. What was going on here? Wasn't it too early for the hunting season?

The next thing I saw was my mother nervously pacing the porch, back and forth. Forth and back. For goodness' sakes, what in tarnation was going on? Suddenly I understood exactly what was going on.

"Ma!" I called out, breaking into a run. The loud yapping of the dogs drowned out my call. "Ma! Hey!!" Still she didn't hear me, but the dogs sure enough did. Their barks grew so insistent that it sounded like they were signaling an end to the world.

As I raced past my brother, he looked as though he was witnessing one of them Bible miracles that the Reverend Ross was always talking about.

With a single leap, I sailed up the three wooden porch steps. "Ma—hey! It's me." For a moment, she just stared at me, then she suddenly wrapped herself around me as tightly as a paper wrapper around a Tootsie Roll.

"Beth! Honey, is you okay? You is well?"

"I'm fine, Ma, honest."

After I said that, she unwrapped me and placed her hands firmly against her wide hips. "Where you think you've been, girl? Getting us worried half out of our minds?"

Using his muscular right arm like a pole, Pa vaulted over the porch's wood railing. "I saw you come running home like the devil was pursuing your soul. What happened to you, Beth? Where you been keeping yourself all through the night?"

As I tried to give Pa an answer to his question, Fancy Annie came rushing onto the porch, looking for all the world like she'd been crying. But that don't make sense 'cause any girl who's liked by both Jason Savage and Herbie Ferrell couldn't find much of anything to cry about. Could she? "You is home, Beth," she said, just as though she had to say it to believe it.

I saw that my pa and my ma were still waiting for my answer. "Where I was," I said, looking anywhere but at their faces, "was in hiding. Reckon I felt so ashamed that I couldn't stand to be seen—not even by the man in the moon!"

The men and their dogs began gathering around the porch. Hooking both his thumbs through his belt loops, Pa strode forward. As he did, the men and their animals seemed to quiet down. "'Cause of what happened under the Old Rugged Cross Church tent last night, our girl needed to be off by herself for a spell. But she's home now, and we praise the Lord for that. And we praise the Lord for all you neighbors and friends too, 'cause when we needed you all, you came running over here, ready and willing to help us. God bless you all."

"That's what neighbors are for, Eugene," called out a voice from the crowd. The men began moving off toward their dusty vehicles, but before they drove off, I heard another man's voice call out, "Prize or no prize, you is still the best leader, Beth Lambert."

After that I went right to my room. Even though it hadn't been much more than an hour since the morning sun rose up, I could hardly wait to throw back my patchwork quilt and crawl wearily into bed. Damp and chilly forest ground ain't the best place for sleeping.

Ma came into my bedroom to tuck me in just like she used to do when I was little. For a while she just stood hovering over my bed and I saw that her silence was heavy with thought. Then she patted my shoulder. "Nobody likes folks who are puffed and folks who are stuffed. Reckon you've learned what happens to them that is all blown up with pride?" But without waiting for me to speak, she plunged headlong into her answer. "Same thing that happened to Humpty Dumpty. That's what!"

But truth to tell, I wasn't much listening to her. Instead I was thinking about what I now had to do. 'Cause when a person fails in full view of everybody that's important to her, then something has got to be done. Something spectacular to make up for the shame. All my friends may now be thinking that I'm just some poor, old laughable thing, but I'm not. I'm still their leader, the best one around!

Ma gave me a grateful hug. "So I reckon that after everything that's happened, you've already reached up to the Lord to ask for more guidance and wisdom."

"Ma'am?" I asked, hoping that she wouldn't get the idea that I hadn't been paying close attention.

"Just asking you, Beth babe, what is your plans now that you've had time for a talk with the Lord, asking him to grant you wisdom?"

"Well, what I plan . . ." I said, suddenly feeling a rush of power within me. So much power that all by myself I could light up the skies of Pocahontas and maybe even farther! Why, with all this energy I do believe that I could be an independent power source to all of Randolph County.

"What I plan," I repeated, "is something bigger and better than I've ever planned before. Something so important that even years from now, folks will still be talking about it."

"I don't think I'm hearing right!" said Ma, placing her fingers into her ears just as though she didn't want to hear.

her as I moved off toward the bedroom. "Seems like you're not one bit listening when the Reverend Ross stands up in church to preach on the need for trust."

Ma appeared at the door, wiping her hands on the skirt of her flowered apron. "Reckon you could help me lay aside my suspicions?"

"Would it make you feel any better if I told you that I'm going to become coach of a championship relay-racing team?"

Her suspicions didn't seem to totally fade. "Never known you to run when you could walk . . . and come to think of it, I've never known you to walk when you could ride."

"Maybe running ain't my favorite thing in all this world, but being the coach and captain of the championship relay-racing team is sure enough going to be one of my favorite things."

Shaking her head, Ma went off toward the kitchen while I laid my baby brother on the table and undid the large safety pins at his waist. "This is some wet diaper, sure enough," I told him as I slipped off the dripping cloth and washed him with a warm soapy cloth. Baby Benjamin made joyful sounds the whole time I patted him dry with a striped terry-cloth towel that had already begun to grow bald.

A shake or two from a can of powder made him look as though he had come into the world a brown-skinned, white polka-dotted baby. But with his lower lip pressed forward like it was, he looked to me like an old wise man in the midst of making a decision that would affect something every bit as important as the whirling and twirling of the planet Earth.

At least this moment, I felt as though I could tell him things that nobody else could possibly understand. "You think it's fair of the Reverend Ross doing what he did?" I found myself asking him. "Giving my Abner Brady Award to Philip Hall? Bet things would have been different if I was born a Bob instead of a Beth. Or if it had been the Reverend Ross's wife giving out the *Agnes* Brady Award.

"And why is it when a boy does a little bragging, folks just laugh and say that he's behaving like a boy? But let a girl do it and any laughing that you find won't be the good-natured kind.

"Don't know why I'm telling all this stuff to a baby. Besides, nobody who's only been on this earth for only two hundred days could possibly understand what it's like to make a total and complete public fool of themselves.

"Can you even guess, Baby Benjamin, what it feels like, when you walk into the Busy Bee Bargain Store or the post office and hear people laughing, to suspect that they're laughing at you? Just a-talking and a-laughing about what happened last Sunday night."

I reached for a fresh diaper. "So what do you have to say about all of this, you sweet thing?" Baby Benjamin opened his mouth. Was he going to say his first word?

"AHHHHH!" I screamed, for suddenly I'd been struck directly in the face by a forceful stream of warm pee!

"Benjamin! Baby Benjamin! How could you do such a thing to someone who loves you!?" I asked. He only looked pleased with himself, giggling as though he had just discovered a new and wonderful game.

Mr. Simon Blake's well-worn green pickup truck moved swiftly along our narrow rutted road, stirring up a cloud of flying dust particles. At our porch the truck's engine was abruptly cut. Bonnie was the first to jump from the back platform, followed by Esther, Susan, and Ginny, who actually may have been a little bit gorgeous.

"You can bring on the apples, Ma," I called through the screen door, thinking that now, at last, with a little help from the Pennies, I was going to achieve a success so great that nobody—absolutely nobody—would ever again remember my shameful night of the Abner Brady.

As soon as I accomplish my objective, this town is going to be impressed with me all over again. Why, some folks might even think it's a good idea to do something really special in my honor. Maybe a banquet in the church with real cloth napkins or even a barn-size, five-color neon sign strung up across Main Street announcing to the world:

Pocahontas, Arkansas,

is proud as peaches

of

ELIZABETH LORRAINE LAMBERT,

our

Finest Leader!

Reckon it's going to take a heap of effort to deserve a sign like that, but there ain't no effort that would be too much trouble. Not if it will stop the laughing.

My six-foot-tall brother walked out onto the porch, looking as spiffy as a preacher on revival night. "How you all doing, Ginny?"

But it was Bonnie who answered. "You sure is looking nice tonight, Luther Lambert."

The only answer that Luther gave was an up-and-down slide of his adam's apple. Just then Esther tugged at the sleeve of my denim jacket. "What's all this here mystery about, Beth? How come you wouldn't tell us what the emergency is? I don't feel right not knowing what the emergency is. You going to tell us now?"

Bonnie spoke from the corner of her mouth. "Maybe Beth has decided to teach us all how to win Mister Abner Brady's award."

The Pennies found Bonnie's humor so irresistible that even after I called for quiet, they went right on laughing. I stood there feeling as though I wanted to go into hiding again. But all I did was smile, pretending that I too was enjoying everybody's good spirits.

Probably because I didn't seem to be even a little bit upset with the laughter, they soon wearied of it. Then they made themselves comfortable on the porch swing while I leaned up against the railing. And I got to thinking that my friends weren't what you'd call bad friends, it was just that they'd never learned how to feel somebody else's pain.

By the time everybody had finished eating their baked cinnamon apple, the twilight had already deepened into night. I lit the porch's kerosene lamp and then rapped authoritatively for quiet against the pine table. "This here emergency meeting of the Pretty Pennies Girls Club of Pocahontas, Arkansas, is now called to order."

"Finally the mystery is going to be solved," said Esther with a sigh. "I couldn't for the life of me think of any emergency big enough to call an emergency meeting for. I thought about it, but I couldn't, not for the life of me—"

Again I rapped my knuckles on the table for quiet. "Esther, you is interrupting your president and chief presiding officer while she is a-speaking."

"Why, you wasn't doing no speck of speaking!" she insisted. "Anyway, I only talked in a little of the space that you wasn't using."

I threw my arms into the air. "Ain't you all interested in the biggest thing that's going to happen to this here

29

town since Pocahontas's own Wanda Jane Scubbins represented Arkansas in the Miss America Contest?!"

Susan broke into song. "There she is . . . Miss A-mer-i-ca . . ."

"Her being in the contest was what happened way back when my mama was a girl," said Bonnie. "And anyways this year's contest done already come and gone."

"I ain't talking nothing about no Miss America Contest!" I told her.

"Why, I heard you plain as day," insisted Bonnie, while all the other Pennies nodded their heads in agreement. "Talking to us about how Wanda Jane Scubbins went up to Atlantic City to win the Miss America Contest. Only, as any fool can tell you, Wanda Jane didn't win. And that's how come Pocahontas ain't what you'd call a famous place like Little Rock or New York!"

I sighed like grown-ups sometimes do when they have to explain complicated things to young children. "I wasn't talking about the Miss America Contest, I was only using it as an example 'cause that happened way back before Wanda Jane Scubbins married up with Mr. Timothy Flood, who owns the Flood Ford Company."

"My mother remembers her when she was still Wanda Jane Scubbins," added Susan. " 'Cause they was exactly the same age then. Reckon," she said after a pause, "that they is still exactly the same age, only now it's a different age."

"This meeting will come to order!" I said, smacking the table with such force that a terrible pain shot through my hand. "I called this meeting for a very important purpose and so I don't want to hear no more of nothing about Wanda Jane."

"Well, I for one think it's mighty interesting," said Bonnie Blake. "A whole heap more interesting than this here emergency of yours which looks like no emergency to me."

"If that's what you think, Bonnie, then why did you bother to come to the meeting? And if the rest of you have your minds all made up like poor ole Bonnie here, then you are all wasting my time. And since you've already had your refreshments, I might as well adjourn this meeting."

"I came to hear about the emergency!" said Esther.

Ginny told Bonnie to be quiet and then looked directly at me. "My mind ain't one bit made up."

Like hungry turkeys they pressed their necks forward. At last I had won their attention. "I called this meeting to tell you all that them Tiger Hunters are always going around saying that they are something while we Pretty Pennies ain't much of nothing."

Bonnie looked especially disturbed. "They been saying that? About us?"

I prayed that what I was telling them was true, but if it wasn't I prayed the Lord would find it in his heart to forgive me. I had to give the Pennies a reason to want to beat the Tigers even though it wouldn't have to be the only reason. I knew not one of them could understand why I'd never feel good again until I could make up for the Abner Brady.

"That's what them boys been saying," I said, pausing long enough for all the Pennies to be stung by that thought. "And what we've got to do is to prove to them that Pennies can do anything Hunters can do, only better!"

"How you reckon we is going to prove that?" asked Esther.

"Oh, we'll prove it," I said, trying to sound mysterious. "We'll prove it to everybody."

Bonnie, Esther, Ginny, and Susan looked at each other just as though they were all lost.

"Those Tiger Hunters," I explained, "have been going around for so long saying they is faster runners than us Pretty Pennies that they got half the folks in this town believing it. That's why we've got to save our honor. We've got to publicly challenge them to a relay race."

"Well, if we had raced last summer at the church picnic," said Bonnie, "instead of spending what was to be our racing time hunting for Phil, then everybody in this town might know for sure that they really are faster."

Slowly, very slowly I shook my head. "I hope that none of the rest of you is so weak and ailing in spirit."

"Have you looked at their legs lately?" asked Ginny.

"It's bad enough just looking at their faces!" said Susan, making a face like she had bitten into a sour pickle.

Ginny went right back to the subject. "Them boys got themselves some mighty long-looking legs."

"Why, that's nothing to worry about," I told them all. " 'Cause we're going to be trained by a relay-racing expert. But first let me tell you all about what's going to happen at the most exciting relay race that Randolph County has ever seen. Now the way I plan it is that all up and down Main Street, giant banners will be waving high in the wind." Funny thing was, in my mind I could already see them waving.

I went on. "And those banners going to tell everybody about the great contest between the Pennies and the Hunters. Folks from all over Randolph County will crowd into our town while Miss Ramona Thomas will be busy making a permanent record of it for *The Pocahontas Weekly News.*"

There was a clap or two. "Getting our picture in the paper is a lot like being famous!" said Susan.

I raised my hands for quiet, but the Pennies couldn't stop talking because they had two irresistible topics under discussion: becoming famous and the length of a Tiger Hunter's leg.

I had to scream for quiet twice before they stopped. "Oh, there's a lot more to a relay race than just the racing. First, we're going to have us a fine parade led by the Pine Bluff All-Girl Drum and Bugle Corps, and they're going to be followed by two bands."

"Two bands?" repeated Susan.

"Two bands are twice as nice as one," I told her. "And after that Sheriff Miller will shoot his gun from the middle of Main Street to begin the relay race. Mr. Putterham will be there too, waiting to present a Putterham prize to each Pretty Penny for her winning race."

"Could you tell us which Mr. Putterham you is referring to?" asked Bonnie.

"The only Mr. Putterham that we have ever known. The one and only Mr. Cyrus J. Putterham, sole owner and operator of the Busy Bee Bargain Store!"

All the Pennies got busy poking each other and giggling just like I was asking them to believe in fairy tales. Bonnie began laughing so hard that the tears ran down her cheek. But somehow it didn't bother me 'cause this time they weren't laughing at me.

Bonnie wiped away her tears with the back of her hand. "Why, that mean old man Putterham wouldn't give nothing away for free . . . not even a summer cold."

"Well, this time things will be different, because we're going to find that man a good reason to be generous."

A couple of the Pennies broke into enthusiastic applause, and I waited until the clapping died away. "Please remember this: The prizes ain't even the best part," I said.

"Well, what could be better'n a prize?" asked Susan.

When you really know something, the answer comes easy. "Better'n a prize is once and for all proving to them Tiger Hunters and everybody else in this town that I—I mean that all us Pennies—shouldn't be laughed at, because we're all worth more than anybody thinks." And even before we began chanting our official club chant, I could tell by their faces that they believed in what I said, that once again they believed in me.

Go, Pret-ty Pen-nies . . .
Go, Pret-ty Pen-nies . . .
Go, Pret-ty Pen-nies . . .
GO! GO! GO!

Right off I took advantage of the enthusiasm and began singing out orders. "Bonnie, you're such a good talker that I'm putting you in charge of publicity. Congratulations! You're our new publicity chief."

"I don't know nothing about no publicity."

"All you have to do is two things," I explained. "Go on down to *The Pocahontas Weekly News* and talk to Miss Ramona Thomas. Tell her all about our plans for the biggest, most exciting day that this town has ever seen. Tell Miss Ramona that we're scheduling our race for Saturday, October twentieth."

"That's no good," said Bonnie. " 'Cause the third Saturday in October is always taken up with Dollar Day in Pocahontas."

"That's exactly the day we have to have it. On Dollar

35

Day when Pocahontas is filled up with folks who come into town for the bargains."

Bonnie looked as though she was beginning to understand. "Well, what's the second thing?"

"The second thing is to have a talk with the Reverend Ross about what we're doing and let him know how the Old Rugged Cross Church can help."

"How can the church help us race?" said Bonnie.

"By asking the bands to perform and the businesses to give away prizes. Because, you see, nobody, not even the devil himself, wants to say no to a church."

Then I informed Susan that I was placing her in complete charge of our relay-racing uniforms. "Champions have got to look like champions," I told her. "Since you sew so good, all you have to do is to make up five matching uniforms. They have to be comfortable enough for running, pretty to look at, and cost about free."

Susan pushed out her lower lip. "What do I look like to you, Beth, your fairy godmother?"

"I wouldn't have as much confidence in Cinderella's own personal fairy godmother as I have in you, Susan," I said, turning my attention to another Penny. "Esther, it's going to be your job to talk with those Tiger Hunters. Tell them that we hereby challenge them to the race of the century. A race we aim to win. Then see if you all can agree on a route. Don't much matter what the route is, 'cause anything you decide upon will be mighty fine with me, just as long as it begins at the pitcher show and ends in front of Mr. Cyrus J. Putterham's Busy Bee Bargain Store."

Esther, who isn't much of a talker, threw me a proper-looking salute.

"And Ginny, it's going to be your responsibility to find the three most fair-minded folks in all of Pocahontas. Find them and ask them to judge our race."

She looked surprised. "You mean you're going to let me choose the judges?"

"I have all the confidence in the world in you. Naturally, though, I know who you're going to choose."

Ginny's gorgeous face held enough wonder for two. "You do?"

"Certainly, 'cause you is wise enough to only choose people who are fair, honest, and just a-brimming over with integrity," I told her. "And since Sheriff Nathan Miller, Miss Eleanor Linwood, and Miss Ramona Thomas best fit that description, I reckon that's who you're going to choose."

Nodding in agreement, Ginny smiled her sweetest.

"And because we all know how much Bonnie loves singing and dancing and things that are happy, I hereby bestow upon Bonnie Blake the high honor of having a second responsibility. Besides being director of publicity, she will also be our parade director!"

"Parade director?" Bonnie squealed with delight. "Oh, I loves parading even more than I loves relay racing."

"First comes the parade and then comes the race," I explained. "Tell the Pine Bluff All-Girl Drum and Bugle Corps that they can lead off our parade followed by the Paragould Veterans of Foreign Wars Band and I reckon we'll end up with our own Pocahontas High School Band. Tell all them bands that that's exactly the order you want them to march. No switching around! Just remember that you, Bonnie Blake, are going to be directing this parade and things got to be done your way. Exactly your way! You hear?"

Bonnie looked dreamily off into the distance while she spoke, which made it seem her next words were meant for nobody but herself.

"Seems like all my older brothers and sisters get to make decisions. But me? I never get to make no decisions. Leastways, I never did until my baby sister, Evelyn Rose, got her hair caught in the wringer washing machine."

For a thoughtful moment, our parade director examined the nail of her right index finger.

"If I had made the wrong decision about which way to pull the lever, then that ole roller would have pulled out every strand of that little girl's hair. So I figured and figured but finally I figured right!"

"How come you didn't pull the electrical cord and save yourself all that figuring?" I asked.

As Bonnie began a stammering defense of exactly why she hadn't taken the more direct method, I found myself feeling sorry for her. Nobody had asked for my advice.

I tried to think of some merciful way to change the subject.

"And now the last job goes to Esther," I said, deciding to give it to her then and there. "Because Esther's sweet talk is just a little bit sweeter than anybody else's. And that's why I'm giving her a second job, which carries with it the title Chief of the Putterham Prizes!"

"Well, what is you talking about now, Beth?" called out Bonnie. "I've lived around these parts all my life and I ain't never heard tell of no Putterham prizes."

If it hadn't been for the fact that I was still feeling sorry about the humiliation that I caused her, I probably would have answered her back with my sassiest voice—the voice that Luther says is someday going to be ruled illegal. But I didn't. "Well, we're all glad that your life ain't hardly over yet."

"Reckon I can sweet-talk a little," admitted Esther. "But I ain't never heard about any Putterham prizes either, and a man as mean, ornery, and stingy as old Putterham is going to need stronger medicine than a little sweet talk."

"Don't you think Mr. Putterham would like to have his store advertised?" I asked. "All during relay-race day, a lot of folks will be coming into town to shop on Dollar Day and to watch the race. Best day of the year to advertise. Even a man as bad as the old Putty Dutty can understand that. Even he might think it's okay to spend a little to sell a lot."

"Guess it could work like that," said Esther, still looking a little uncertain.

"I can see it all now," I told them. "With hundreds of folks looking on, Mr. Putterham strides up to the finish line, where we winners are waiting. And while all the watchers are thinking that a man who'd give prizes away isn't such a bad fellow after all, the merchant speaks to the crowd: 'And now on behalf of the best store in all of Randolph County, the Busy Bee Bargain Store where we are running specials on hosiery for the ladies and gabardine work shirts for the men, I hereby and therefore present to each and every Pretty Penny their valuable prize.'"

Even Bonnie Blake was smiling. It was just as though they were all caught up in my vision of our victory. I lifted my hands high above everybody's head the way our preacher does when he gives the benediction. "Everybody's got their work to be doing, so now this emergency meeting is over. Adjourned."

"Don't go calling adjourned," yelled Bonnie. "You left somebody out. How come you didn't give yourself nothing to do?"

"Why Bonniebonniebonnie," I said, shaking my head vigorously as if I was trying to shake her very words from my ears. "When the day comes that your president and chief presiding officer don't do her share of the work, then that's the day you can complain. —Just a minute," I said, waving a thin red book titled *Everything There Is to Know About Relay Racing . . . Plus a Little Bit More* in front of their noses.

"Does that mean that you is going to be our coach, Beth Lambert?" asked Bonnie.

"And not just any old coach," I told her, striking the table with my open palm, "but the coach of the championship team! And so now for the last and final time, this meeting is now and forever . . . adjourned!"

"Well, you better get yourself busy with your coaching," suggested Susan. " 'Cause when it comes to running, them Tiger Hunters ain't half bad."

"Now don't none of you worry about that," I said, slapping the front cover of the book. " 'Cause I think I'll give you all your first lesson right now."

Susan shook her head. "I'm not going to go racing around in the nighttime, tripping over some rock."

I corrected her. "In this particular lesson, we won't have to run. We're just going to learn what to do when we do run. Okay?"

"Okay," agreed at least two Pennies.

"First lesson: At the very beginning of the race, outrun your opponent and that will make him lose confidence. Got that?" I asked. "That ends the first lesson."

"That's all?" asked Bonnie.

"Now don't go being some old worrywart," I told her. " 'Cause when the time comes for running, what is it we Pretty Pennies are going to do?"

"Run," said Esther.

"Let's hear it from everybody."

They all called back in unison, "Run!"

I screamed at them, "Shout it like you mean it!"

"RUN! RUN! RUN!"

Chapter 3

The relay race

For the last three weeks, ever since the emergency meeting, I've been sleeping a worried sleep. So many things on my mind. Have to check to see that the route of the race is clearly marked. And there should be chairs for the judges. All the judges deserve their own chairs. Did Susan finish sewing the last running suit? Did Esther wrap all the Putterham prizes? With bows?

We tried keeping the prizes a secret. At first only Susan and I knew that all the members of the winning team will be given their own Ouija boards, but now all the Pennies know and maybe even the Hunters know too.

As I threw my quilt back and sat upright in bed, I told myself not to worry. Why, I've personally seen to a thousand—no, a million details. Outside of the coaching, which I'm going to do today, everything I could think to do, I did. And a lot of other people pitched in too. Every time we Pennies needed help, didn't the ladies of the Old Rugged Cross Sisterhood do what they could? Since all those things are true, I told myself I absolutely had nothing to fret about. Yes, but the truth was I was fretting—fretting a whole lot. I looked out my bedroom window, surprised to see that a day as special as this one looked an awful lot like any other cool October morning.

Luther was already at the table, his long legs poking out from beneath the flowered oilcloth. Ma placed a plate of buckwheat pancakes in front of him. Without looking up as he poured on the syrup, he spoke. "You keep a secret?"

"Why you know good and well I can!" I answered, feeling proud that somebody as strong and as smart as Luther Lambert would share a secret with me.

"The guys—Herbie Ferrell and Jason Savage and all the rest of them—would kid me if they knew, but well . . . well, I'm rooting for you."

Ma placed a heaping stack of her hot pancakes in

front of me. "Nobody could have worked any harder for this day than our Beth here. Don't think she ever once stopped working on making this day a success."

I heard my mother's words, but somehow I was a lot more thrilled by my brother's. From Ma I get a good many words of encouragement, but from Luther encouraging words were as rare as an Arkansas snowstorm. "Really, you are rooting for me, Luther? Really and truly?" I asked, not because I doubted his words, but because I wanted to hear him say them again. Then if he wanted to, he could go on and tell me he hadn't lost one speck of confidence in me either just because of some silly old not-worth-remembering Abner Brady night.

Maybe he'd even say those words he said to me the time he was running a fever and I had to take care of his precious pigs. That's when he looked me right in the eye and said those thrilling words I'll never forget: "For a kid sister, Beth, you ain't half bad."

But when he began to eat a forkful of pancake, I knew that there were no more pretty words a-coming.

By midmorning, Pa and Luther had come back from the fields. Their blue-denim overalls were earth stained and their foreheads were edged with tiny drops of sweat. Pa gave his firstborn a jab to the shoulder. "Reckon we ought to leave the womenfolk at home, Luther? Your ma there is having so much fun cooking and your sisters are having so much fun a-washing and a-cleaning that it don't hardly seem right to interrupt them."

Luther quickly nodded his agreement. "That's right thoughtful of you, Pa, 'cause none of them would want to go into Pocahontas just to watch a relay race."

Fancy Annie and I both moaned out, "Oh, Pa. . . ." But my mother just rolled her eyes and gently shook her head like she did whenever Pa teased.

It was still on the morning side of noon when all of us shined and scrubbed Lamberts climbed aboard the pickup truck and headed north on Highway 67 toward the big—P. Pocahontas, U.S.A.!

Seemed as though Pa too could hardly wait to get there, 'cause he was driving fast enough to excite the frisky October wind. Where I sat on the back of the truck I could feel it zip through the cherry-red running suit that Susan had made from an old Fairy Flake Flour sack. But I didn't care if I was chilled, 'cause every single turkey-pimple (Pa insists that as long as we make our living off the turkey, we shouldn't be giving all the glory to the goose) seemed to shout at me to wake and come alive. ALIVE!

After the Pennies' victory today, I'd probably be hoisted high on the shoulders of grateful Pocahontians and cheered from one end of Main Street to the other. Not only was I going to return to being the leader I used to be, but after today I'd be looked upon as better than ever, the best leader in all of Randolph County. Yep, today was going to be it. A day among days!

As the Lambert Farm truck turned onto Main Street

Ma tapped the rear window. "That the secret sign you worked so hard on?" she called out.

"That's it!" I yelled proudly, jumping to my feet to salute the red-white-and-black banner billowing high across the town's Main Street:

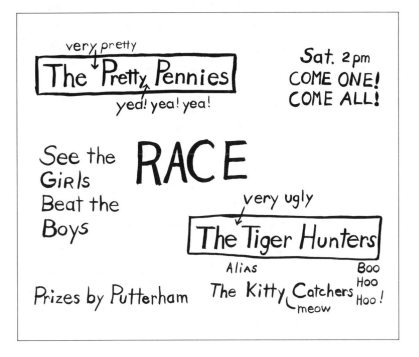

I was thrilled to see just how much more noticeable my sign looked now in the light of day than it had been in yesterday's twilight when Luther helped me string it up.

"It's beautiful!" I shouted. Then Fancy Annie jumped to her feet and we began doing a do-si-do and swing-your-partner-style square dance on the platform of the still-moving vehicle. We didn't stop our dancing until Pa turned and angle parked in front of Randolph County's courthouse. Without taking the time or the breath for a "See you all later," I jumped from the truck's tailgate and rushed into the building. I ran down a flight of steel stairs, through a long corridor, and into a room. On the door was a makeshift sign boldly printed with red crayon:

Relay Race
Official
Command Post
Private Headquarters
Knock before entering
(this means YOU!)

Without knocking, I rushed through the door. Bonnie, our parade director, was busy explaining policy to a uniformed gentleman who was partially wrapped inside a dazzling gold tuba. "No, sir, the reason that the Paragould Veterans Band is second to march doesn't mean that we think you're second best. No, sir!"

Across the room Susan sat cross-legged, elasticizing the final pair of racing shorts. Esther had already festively wrapped the Putterham prizes and was now making last-minute calculations on an elaborate drawing of the relay-race route. And the gorgeous one was engrossed in printing the names of our three fair-minded judges on the three official gold ribbons.

I clapped my hands to call everyone to attention. "Are you all ready for your final relay-racing lesson? —Come on now, let's get moving. Push those tables over to one side. Pull down those window shades. Never can tell when one of them Tiger Hunters might be spying around."

With a swiftness that seemed almost magical, everything became as I had ordered. The Pennies, wearing identical track suits and white gym shoes, lined up in front of me just as respectfully as soldiers. I felt as proud as a general of the army inspecting her troops.

First thing I did was to lead the Pennies through about five minutes of the special leg-limbering exercises that I had read all about in the book *Everything There Is to Know About Relay Racing . . . Plus a Little Bit More.* Actually I really had studied that book—everything but the last chapter or two, when it got boring.

"These exercises," I explained, "are going to make your legs work more efficiently during the big race."

As soon as we finished our exercise, I led them outside. As we walked the four-square-block relay-race route, I pointed out the hole in the pavement on Main Street and the broken branches on Front Street that were hidden beneath bunches of golden October leaves.

Again I reminded them of what I had carefully preached at our last coaching session: the importance of saving steps on the way to the finish line by running as close to the right-hand side of the street as possible.

Back inside the Official Command Post Headquarters, I told the Pennies that I had some final advice for them.

"The last thing I want to talk with you about is pain."

"Pain?" Bonnie repeated just as though she was saying a very long and difficult word.

"Yes, ma'am, Miss Bonnie, pain! 'Cause when you be running as hard as you can for four long blocks, then pain going to be running right along with you. And soon the pain going to begin whispering, 'Ease up your running a little and I promise not to hurt you so bad.' Ain't no mistake about it, that's what the pain is going to be saying. So what you have to decide long before you take your first step is what you're going to say back to the pain."

"How about 'Pain, pain, go away . . . come again another day,'" said Bonnie, laughing as though she had told the funniest joke in this or in any other century.

"What you've got to say," I said, paying not the slightest bit of attention to Bonnie, "is that pain is the price you have to pay for winning. Keep on repeating: 'Pain is the price you have to pay for winning.' "

I left the Pennies to finish up their work and went alone into a day that was cool, but just as bright as anything. On the courthouse green, folks sat about in family-sized bunches, eating homemade sandwiches of cheese, bologna, or ham, and sloshing them down with strawberry Nehis and Dr Peppers.

A large woman, wearing a gray buttoned cardigan sweater over her flowered cotton dress, looked up from the orange she was peeling. "Good luck to you girls! I sure do hope you all beat the stuffings out of them sassy boys."

"I sure hope we do too," I answered. She couldn't possibly know how much I meant it.

Her husband's head jerked backward as though he had been slapped smack across the face. "Hush yourself up, Martha! Ain't no boys worth being called boys going to let a bunch of silly girls beat them!"

Even though it was an hour before the big event, Pocahontas's Main Street was already filling up with people. I wondered how many had come in for the Dollar Day bargains and how many had come especially for the relay race. One thing was for sure: There were more people here than I had ever before seen on the streets of this town. And a lot of them had to come from distant places too, because their faces wasn't familiar.

And crossing Main Street was Miss Ramona Thomas,

walking faster than any other Pocahontian could. Her shoulders were bent slightly forward to balance her weighty camera bag, and the pockets of her jacket were bulging with flashbulbs.

On the west side of the courthouse, enterprising farmers were selling bushels of apples, potatoes (both Irish and sweet), green beans, okra, collards, pecans, and even live speckled hens from the tailgates of their pickup trucks.

Rightly guessing that there would be a lot of folks in town for the great race and Dollar Day, the ladies from the Old Rugged Cross Church had made their own bakesale booth from upturned milk crates covered by flowered oilcloth. And sitting on the oilcloth, as pretty as you please, was a pecan pie that looked like it had more pecans in it than grow on a lot of pecan trees. The apple and rhubarb pies didn't look half bad either, and there were also squares of creamy chocolate fudge that looked good enough to eat.

All along the street women stopped me to pat my shoulder and wish us Pennies good luck. Their menfolk though didn't join in the well-wishing. Instead they acted as though their faces had frozen into ice and their tongues had fallen off from years of nonuse.

In fact Mayor Daniel Lathrup was the only man in Pocahontas who didn't act like a man—I mean he didn't act like all those other men.

When he saw me he rushed over and almost shook my

arm from its socket. "Who but you, Beth, could have
provided our citizens with such a glorious holiday? Why,
this town hasn't seen so much goings-on since Brother
Sidney Spector came here all the way from Cleveland,
Ohio, to lead the revival meetings!"

Suddenly Mayor Lathrup pointed to the first clown I
had ever seen on the streets of any town. His hair was the
color of stewed tomatoes and he carried a large, boldly
painted sign:

DON'T CLOWN AROUND . . .
DO ALL YOUR FAMILY'S SHOPPING AT
THE BUSY BEE BARGAIN STORE!

"Can't talk to you anymore now, Beth," said the mayor.
"I got to go say howdy to that clown before he goes
wasting his time with children."

And if a clown didn't provide proof aplenty that Pocahontas, Arkansas, is a pretty exciting place to be, there
was still more: From the far side of the courthouse green
floated the sound of music. Music like the angels would
play. I didn't need anybody to tell me that Wilfred and
Verna Glenway had arrived all the way from Black
Rock, Arkansas, with their sweet-stringed dulcimers.

I watched them good-looking Glenways strumming
their instruments with finely tapered turkey (they could
have possibly been chicken) quills. "On top of Old
Smoky . . . All covered with snow . . . I lost my true
lover . . . From courting too slow. . . ."

While the Singing Glenways held on to the last note as fiercely as if it had been their last dollar, there was a burst of applause.

"You all make music that God on his throne would be proud to claim," said a lady with a grapefruit-shaped face. "But with all the songs that are waiting to be sung, I was a-thinking and a-wondering how you two ever decide between you what songs to sing and play."

Verna Glenway laughed as she patted the sleeve of Wilfred's plaid cowboy shirt. "Nothing to it. We just sit down, and in a calm and reasonable manner we discuss it. Like I always say, if two people are reasonable, there's never no need to argue."

Then Mrs. Glenway spotted me at the back of the crowd. "Beth? Beth Lambert? —Is that really you?"

"Yes'm," I said, pushing myself between several layers of people. "It sure enough is."

"Well, well, well," she said, shaking my hand and smiling. "Wilfred and I are just plumb tickled pink that you thought to invite us. And I guess you know too that we Singing Glenways are keeping all twenty fingers crossed for you Pretty Pennies."

Suddenly Wilfred flashed ten widely separated fingers. "Well, I reckon that all of us Singing Glenways ain't crossing our fingers for you."

Verna looked at her husband with such force that I feared that her eyeballs might come flying from their sockets. "Wilfred, what *are* you talking about?!"

"What I'm talking about is being a male myself!" he explained. "And males don't go crossing their fingers for no females. Girls might be dumb enough to cross their fingers for the Pennies, but boys being boys are smart enough to only cross their fingers for Hunters. Tried and true, true and blue Tiger Hunters!"

"Wilfred!"

"Well now, honey, I'm just telling you the truth."

"Well! Wilfred!"

"Now, now, Verna honey, stay calm. . . ."

"Well!"

"And reasonable."

After passing beyond the sound of Verna's long-distance-carrying voice, I watched the All-Girl Drum and Bugle Corps of Pine Bluff, Arkansas, step smartly from a yellow bus. With their white skirts and matching military-style jackets featuring double rows of brass buttons, they had to be just about the spiffiest-looking creatures that these eyes of mine ever did see.

By the minute more and more people seemed to be pouring into Pocahontas.

In the dusty window of Rusty Browder's shoe-repair shop a clock with Roman numerals marked the time as one thirty. For a good while now I had walked up and down the street accepting congratulations for giving my hometown a fine celebration. And all this time my head had been empty of fears. But now, only thirty minutes shy of race time, the fears came rushing back.

As I walked back inside the Official Command Post Headquarters I called out the order to "Get ready to march like soldiers." And at precisely a quarter to two o'clock, I led the proud-stepping, red-uniformed Pretty Pennies out of the courthouse door, down the concrete steps, and along Main Street's yellow center line to where the race would begin.

Everybody seemed to take notice of us, and all the women waved or applauded or sometimes both.

As soon as we reached the starting line, our parade director began acting as though it was she who was directing this here parade. Waving her clipboard authoritatively, Bonnie made her way through the marchers, telling them all, "Nobody begins no parading until they get the signal. My signal."

I told Bonnie not to bother her head with *her* signal 'cause I could just as easily give them *my* signal while she sort of watched to see that everybody obeyed. She shook her head as stubbornly as Baby Benjamin does when he refuses to eat another bite.

Then Bonnie looked me straight in the eye and said, "Since I is the parade director, that's what it is I aim to do. Direct this here parade!"

Through the generalized noisiness of an excited crowd came a new and different sound. I whirled around in time to see a grim-faced Philip Hall leading his ragged bunch of Tiger Hunters toward the starting line.

They all wore their everyday day-in and day-out

clothes: blue bib overalls with blue-denim shirts. All except for Philip Hall. The top Tiger Hunter had on neatly pressed khaki pants, a plaid shirt, and the tan jacket that he calls his Windbreaker.

It gave me a shot of confidence to see that all the Hunters had on thick, ankle-high leather work shoes. Now work shoes might be fine and dandy for keeping gooshy pasture mud from a person's feet, but they're far too heavy and cloggy for running. Leastways for any serious running.

"Howdy do, Philip Hall," I said, smiling kindly enough to show him and all them onlooking, bystanding folks what a really good sport I am. He didn't smile back so I guess we all know what kind of a sport he is.

With a face that looked as though it had been chiseled out of rock granite Philip Hall marched straight up to me. "I don't one bit like that sign you got strung up over the highway for all the world to see," he said.

I sassed him right back. "Well, if I were you, I wouldn't let it bother me none 'cause what you look like ain't one bit your fault."

"Thing is that your calling us ugly wasn't the worst thing you called us."

I wondered what could be worse than being called ugly. "No?"

"No! 'Cause even worse is your calling us Tiger Hunters by another name. And what you called us was . . . was Kitty Catchers."

I giggled. "Awww, Philip, I thought you was one boy who could take a joke."

"Some things are jokes," he said, his face becoming thoughtful. "And some things ain't. How would you like it if we Tiger Hunters went around calling you Pretty Pennies by another name?"

This time I really laughed. "Ain't nothing in this wide world that you can call a Pretty Penny excepting what she is: a Pretty Penny."

"Oh, there's always something else," he said, looking slightly mysterious. "Something like a . . . something like an Ugly Cent!"

"An Ugly Cent?" I screamed, refusing to believe what I had heard. "Why, Philip Hall, I'm disappointed in you 'cause you of all people ought to know that there are some things which ain't hardly no laughing matter."

Then the steeple bell of the First Baptist Church of Pocahontas chimed once and then once again. Two o'clock. A mighty cheer went up from the overanxious, tired-of-waiting crowd. Then a woman called out, "Sooner the parade starts, the sooner you can win, Pretty Pennies!"

But Bonnie didn't seem to pay much attention to all the encouragement. She just went on about her business like a person who was plenty used to doing things in her own way, and in her own good time. Hugging her clipboard, she shook her head firmly to the restless crowd and pointed to her borrowed wristwatch. "In your places, everybody," she finally announced, lifting her hand into the air and beginning to count backward from one hundred. From one hundred? "100 . . . 99 . . . 98 . . . 97 . . ."

"Two o'clock has already come and gone," I told her, but being stubborn and all, she just went right on counting.

". . . 81 . . . 80 . . . 79 . . ."

"You going to start up this here parade, girlie?" asked a man—I think it was Mr. Henry Gagnon.

But the only answer coming from Bonnie Blake's lips was "53 . . . 52 . . . 51 . . . 50 . . . 49 . . . 48 . . . 47 . . ."

Gradually more and more people started chanting, "We want our parade, we want our parade." But all that happened was that our parade director's counting got even slower. ". . . 27 . . . . 26 . . . . 25 . . . . 24 . . . . 23 . . . . 22 . . . . 21 . . . ."

More people—men, boys and even some women too—began to chant. I didn't join in the chanting because I figured that it would probably be easier to move mountains than to move Bonnie from the center of attention one second before she was required to leave it.

". . . . . 7 . . . . . 6 . . . . . 5 . . . . . 4 . . . . . 3 . . . . . 2 . . ." And then Bonnie slowly raised a solitary finger heavenward as though she had caught the good Lord doing something naughty. Slowly that finger began to fall until it pointed directly at the Pine Bluff All-Girl Drum and Bugle Corps. "And now, MARCH!" she shouted.

In precise rhythm with their snare drums, the corps

began to move in one great body on down Main Street. Following them was a John Deere tractor that was so factory-fresh I could still smell the red paint. Mr. Albert Finn of Finn's Farm Equipment Center drove with his right hand while throwing silver-foiled candy Kisses into the crowd with his left. "Thanks for inviting me to the parade, Beth," he yelled as he passed me. "Like I always say, what good is a parade without a John Deere tractor leading the way?"

After the tractor came the men of the Paragould Veterans Band sucking in their considerable bellies.

The final two paraders were the Singing Glenways, but they weren't playing their dulcimers. In fact they seemed to be far more interested in the interesting things that they were telling each other.

As they came closer to me, I could hear Verna saying, "For the life of me, I'll never understand how a grown man could say the things that—"

And Wilfred answering, "Now, now, Verna. Be reasonable. Please."

After the last parader had marched the entire mile route and circled back to the courthouse, Mayor Lathrup strode with purposeful steps to the top of the courthouse steps. Once there, he looked leisurely over the huge audience and then raised his hands for quiet.

"Ladies and gentlemen, citizens of Pocahontas, and visitors from neighboring towns, I extend to you all my official greeting. You are as welcome as the rain that ends a summer's drought. This is going to be one fine day for all of us because some people, people like Beth Lambert here, have such a God-given talent for making things exciting." Then he looked directly at me. "Beth planned well and she worked hard and we all thank her for it."

The clapping and cheering that followed the mayor's words were all for me. And it made me feel as though a warm, strong light had just been switched on inside my heart.

When finally my personal clapping fell away, our mayor also thanked the Pocahontas Chamber of Commerce, the Old Rugged Cross Church, the participants, and even Miss Singleton from his own office. Then he introduced the three relay-race judges: Miss Eleanor Linwood, Miss Ramona Thomas, and Sheriff Nathan Miller, all of whom came in for a good round of applause.

But it was the sheriff of Randolph County who was given the honor of explaining the official rules of the race. "Beth Lambert, the captain and coach of the Pretty Pennies, and Phil Hall, captain and coach of the Tiger Hunters, will each, at the firing of my pistol, begin running the town block carrying a red handkerchief." He unsnapped the dark leather gun holster at his waist and took out a nickel-plated revolver that glinted silver as the sun's rays struck it.

Then Miss Linwood and Miss Ramona came down to

the starting line and handed Philip and me identical handkerchiefs. Meanwhile the sheriff went right on with his explaining. "At the firing of my gun, the two captains will race around the block to hand their red banners over to their waiting teammates, who will do exactly the same thing. Et cetera . . . et cetera . . . et cetera. First team completing the five laps will be proclaimed winner. All right, captains, on your MARK!" he called, aiming his weapon at a right friendly-looking puff of a cloud.

I heard the click that cocked the gun. I saw the sheriff squint as though he was taking dead aim on some high-flying far-distant bull's-eye. "GET SET!" he yelled as though he was born into this world with a voice wired for sound. "GO!!"

Then the shot cracked across the heavens to send me racing off. If I don't do anything else in my life, I've got to do this: beat Philip Hall across the finish line, 'cause a Pretty Penny win is going to go a long ways in erasing the still painful memory of the Abner Brady.

I was running faster than anybody had ever before run . . . faster than your ordinary shooting star. My legs weren't legs anymore. They were giant locomotive wheels barreling down well-greased tracks as if there were no force on this earth that could slow them down.

I knew that no other human person had ever before moved with such speed and just maybe no other human person ever would. But maybe the best thing of all was knowing that Philip Hall could only see my swiftly moving back while I (thank the Lord) couldn't see him at all.

As I rounded my first corner (one down and three to go), the effort of the run was no longer pleasurable. But it didn't matter because I wasn't about to slow down. What was that speech I had given the Pennies? About pain being the price you pay for winning?

Turning the second corner (two down, I know I can do two more!), my breath was beginning to come in short, painful spurts. But it didn't matter none because I wasn't going to slow down. No, sir! Didn't I promise myself? And after all, I was winning. I had to win this race!

Again and again I told myself that I wasn't one bit going to slow down as I began to . . . God help me! I was beginning to slow down. Didn't want to . . . had to . . . had to stop the dragon's breath from singeing the insides of my chest with its fire.

As I clutched my chest, the captain of the Kitty Catchers appeared noiselessly at my side. Smiling his widest smile, he called out with what sounded like breath a-plenty:

> *"Oh, Bethy . . .*
> *Oh, Bethy . . .*
> *Full of confetti,*
> *You and your Pennies*
> *Going to get nothing . . .*
> *But sweaty! ! !"*

As we rounded the third corner together, he leaned his head back to laugh, continuing to run with seemingly effortless motion. More than anything, I wanted to return his insult with one of my own, but my spent body couldn't afford the extra effort, for my lungs felt as though they had long since given up breathing oxygen for kerosene.

Straight ahead was the finish line. Faces. Faces. Never saw so many faces. Shouting . . . cheering . . . faces. "Come on! Come on!" Who are they cheering for?

Philip Hall moved a little ahead of me and then a little bit more. That's when I remembered that running was not the best thing that I did.

The space between Philip Hall and me grew steadily larger. The screaming from the finish line became louder and more insistent. He hasn't won yet, I told myself. Lots of things could happen to a Tiger Hunter on his way to the finish line.

I tried concentrating on pleasant thoughts to take my mind off the burning in my chest. Remembering a bedtime story that my mother used to tell. About a tortoise and a hare. Funny time to be thinking about bedtime stories. Move those legs. Got to keep them moving. MOVE!

In the next moment it was going to happen and there was nothing on God's green earth that I could do to prevent it. And then what was going to happen did: I watched as Philip Hall raced across the finish line and handed over the red banner to Jordan Jones, who was already in motion.

From the crowd came a mighty masculine roar.

What wouldn't I give for a stray bolt of lightning to come zipping out of the cloudless sky to strike me down dead. POW! Oh, what wouldn't I give to be that lucky? Suddenly I had an impulse. An impulse born out of desperation. "Catch, Bonnie!" I called, throwing the wadded-up handkerchief toward Bonnie Blake, our second runner. It fell to the ground, but right away she picked it up and began running.

Bonnie could do it, I thought, she could catch up with Jordan Jones. Maybe, just maybe, the Tiger Hunters hadn't won this race. Not yet!

"HALT!" shouted a voice with unquestionable authority. Then there was a crack of gunfire. Sheriff Miller rushed to the middle of the street to wave back one of the runners. It was Bonnie. Why? Confused, she stood for long moments in the middle of Main Street watching Jordan Jones zip around the first corner. Then at last she obeyed the sheriff's command to return to the starting line.

Cupping his hands around his mouth so everybody could hear, Sheriff Nathan Miller explained, "We judges have decided that the rules of the game have been violated. The banner has to be passed *by hand* from runner to runner. Beth Lambert did not do this; she threw the banner. Beth Lambert, will you kindly return to the starting line and actually *hand* the banner to your second runner?

Painfully aware of the laughter and hoots of the men and the groans of the women, I ran over to where Bonnie waited with her hands on her hips and blood in her eyes. Careful to avoid her eyes, I took the handkerchief from her and quickly returned it.

Then without really wanting to, I glanced up at her face. Her expression was so filled with violence that it surprised me Sheriff Miller didn't immediately press charges. Nonetheless Bonnie Blake turned around and began running with her whole heart, a race that was already lost. A race that I had lost singlehandedly, without a bit of help from anybody.

Since I could no longer bear to watch, I moved back behind the crowd and leaned up against the cool brick of the Busy Bee Bargain Store. Only thing that I knew for certain was how much I wanted this awful race to end. Stop. Cease. HALT! I didn't even bother praying for one of them Bible miracles that the Reverend Ross is always talking about. Reckon I didn't pray because I knew no God worth the name would waste one of his hard-to-get miracles on the awful likes of me.

"Come on, Jordan! Get a move on you, boy!" came the cheers from the finish line. Sounded like there wasn't a male voice in all of Randolph County that wasn't cheering Mr. Jordan Jones.

Half a lifetime later, a single high-voiced lady sang

66

out, "Yea, Bonnie!" but she was the only cheerer. Just seems like folks ain't all that interested in clapping for somebody else's losing efforts.

No sooner had Bonnie crossed over the chalked line than Jordan's twin, Joshua, came in. They had three runners in to our two. Suddenly I hated mathematics. At least this particular set of numbers.

I closed my eyes and plugged my ears with my fingers. But I could not keep from hearing. The periodic cheers of the men still came through even though I could no longer tell exactly who they were cheering for. Reckon it was enough to know that it was for the boys . . . only for the boys.

Then there was a crack of gunfire loud enough to send shock waves bouncing around the heavens. And if the combined voices of the men and boys of Randolph County had sounded loud before, now they were deafening. Well, let them yell and let them shout. For all I care they can shout their dang fool heads off.

When the hysteria lessened slightly, Sheriff Nathan Miller called out, "Let's hear it for the Tiger Hunters!"

And voices stronger than all outdoors responded. "Yea TIGER! Yea HUNTERS! Yea, yea TIGER HUNTERS!!"

Then a dumbly grinning Philip Hall was hoisted high upon the shoulders of his grateful townsmen just as though it was none other than Mr. Philip Hall himself who had, once and for all, put an end to the boll weevil, tooth decay, and the multiplication tables.

"Yea PHIL! Yea HALL! Yea, yea PHIL HALL!!"

Well, no wonder they're cheering him. I don't blame them a bit. He's achieved victory and what is it that I have done? I, Beth Lambert, have singlehandedly let down my club, my family, and maybe even every woman and girl in Randolph County. How come I didn't know all the rules? And why, oh why is it that I can never manage to do anything right?

If only I could go back in time. If only I could read the whole book and learn the rules so good that no matter how desperate I became, I would never forget the rules. Throwing the banner! Will I ever live long enough to forget that I, Elizabeth Lorraine Lambert, threw the banner?

With Philip Hall and the rest of the Tiger Hunters still being carried around like winning warriors, the Paragould Veterans Band struck up, "For he's a jolly good fellow . . . for he's a jolly good fellow . . . for he's a jolly good fellow . . . which nobody can deny. . . ."

I went searching for my ma and my pa through the biggest crowd that Pocahontas, Arkansas, had ever seen. I knew that they'd be every bit as eager to leave this public scene of humiliation as me.

But the first person I came face to face with was Bonnie Blake—the very last person in this world I wanted to see. She shot me a look that right away told me that it had been a long time since she had laid her eyes on any sight even half as disgusting as the sight she was at this moment gazing upon: me.

"Guess I don't have to tell you of all people what you did," she said while the other Pennies seemed suddenly to materialize behind her. Each of them wore an expression that nobody would ever mistake as pleasant.

I shook my head. "Reckon you don't."

"Well, what you did," she said, telling me anyway, "when you threw that banner was about the dumbest thing that I've ever in my life heard."

I wanted to say I was sorry, but I didn't because "sorry" seemed like too little a word to even begin to be able to cover the immense size of my crime. So instead I just said, "I know," and then I turned and ran away as fast as I could from all those disdainful eyes.

Finally I spotted my folks leaning up against one of the courthouse's white columns singing "Let Me Call You Sweetheart" with the Paragould Veterans Band. I waited till the song ended before asking, "You all about ready to go on home?"

"Go back home? Now? But why?" Ma asked. "This here is the best fun your pa and I've had in this ole town since they gave a party with fireworks for Wanda Jane Scubbins. That was before she left for Atlantic City."

I sighed. "That was twenty years ago."

She brightened as though my words had somehow proved her point. "When it's that long a spell between the good times, best you better just lean yourself back and enjoy them when they do come."

Suddenly Pa pointed over to the far right-hand side of the courthouse green. "Looky over there, Beth! Ain't them the Pennies and the Hunters squaring off for square dancing?"

"I don't know what dumb thing they're doing."

"That sounds to me like our Beth is eating her heart out," said Ma, seeking my eyes. "Is you all that upset just 'cause the Pennies didn't win?"

"I ain't upset," I shouted, "about nothing in this world!" Suddenly people were turning to look at me. "You think I care anything at all about some stupid relay race?" The muscles of my throat tightened and my eyes burned like they do when kitchen smoke touches them. "Well, I don't! Not a bit!" My voice was rising and I felt embarrassed that I couldn't even control my own voice. "I thought you, Ma, of all people, understood that!"

Trying to force back the tears, I whirled around and began maneuvering through the press of people. Suddenly my hand was grasped and shaken by an elderly lady—a lady whose face I knew even if I couldn't, at that moment, remember her name. "You is one youngun that I want to give my thanks. Sure do, 'cause I've lived hereabouts for a lot of years and I've heard tell of clowns and parades, but I ain't never in my life seen any. Not until now!"

"Yes'm," I answered, working to loosen her hold on my hand. Farther down the concrete steps of the court-house I passed Miss Eleanor Linwood, who flashed her winningest smile. "Oh, it's a great day for Pocahontas, Beth!"

I heard myself answer, "Yes'm," for the second time within the same minute. "Yes'm" is what I said all right, but what I was thinking was that with luck in fifty years every Pocahontian will either have forgotten or forgiven.

That is every Pocahontian excepting one. 'Cause fifty or even a hundred years won't be nearly time enough for me to forgive myself for what I had done here today.

Chapter 4

The secret meeting

Even though the early Monday wind was damp and stinging, I wasn't one bit looking forward to boarding the warm school bus that was now hightailing it down the road toward me. With all the skill of one of them racing-car drivers, Mr. Barnes stopped the big, old vehicle directly in front of me.

The yellow door swung open and I took a deep breath before stepping aboard. For the last eight days—ever since the relay race—I had trained my eyes not to look up. Look nowhere but down. But when I actually climbed aboard without anyone taking special notice, I began to wonder if just maybe they were no longer angry.

Maybe Mama is right when she says that "The Pennies ain't going to be mad at you forever. May seem like forever, but they is going to sooner or later come around."

Then from the rear of the bus a familiar voice shrilled out, "What can you throw besides banners, Beth?" Bonnie Blake's joke was rewarded by giggles from around and about the bus.

"Careful or you might get mixed up and throw your head instead of your banner," added Ginny, and this time Mr. Barnes's old bus rang with a screechy kind of laughter.

When the last school bell of the day finally rang, Miss Johnson motioned for me to come to her desk.

"Yes'm?"

"Beth, about the oral report you gave today on the Pilgrim's colony at Plymouth."

"Yes, ma'am?"

"Well, unfortunately, it wasn't a good report. Certainly way below your usual high standards."

"Yes, ma'am," I said again. It was just about the only thing I could think to answer.

Miss Johnson removed her glasses like she sometimes does when she really wants to see. "All week long you've been acting as though you haven't enough energy to do your own breathing. I don't know who you've been, but you undoubtedly haven't been Beth."

I thought about telling Miss Johnson that I don't care about that because I didn't ever again want to act like me. Who in their right mind would want to be the way I used to be? But I didn't because I felt too tired for any serious discussion. "Yes, ma'am" is all I said. One thing I've learned is that agreeable conversations usually take less time than disagreeable conversations. It was getting late and either with me or without me Mr. Barnes and the school bus would soon be leaving.

Miss Johnson tapped her fingers along the edge of her oak desk. "Actually the main thing wrong with your Pilgrim talk wasn't your facts or even your figures. The major problem is that your talk was mighty boring. Guess the one thing that I never thought I'd live to see was a boring anything by Beth Lambert!"

On the school ground, the gusty wind sent some golden leaves spinning. I pulled my green jacket tight around my body and told myself that walking the three miles home would be less painful than boarding that bus.

But as I walked toward the parking lot I saw Bus Number 5 hadn't as yet left its space.

Toward the back of the bus where all the Pennies liked to congregate, there was still an empty seat left next to Bonnie. I slid in, careful to keep my eyes on the rubber-ribbed flooring. But before I even had a chance to say hi, Bonnie was already making a suggestion. "Since every-

body here knows how much Beth loves relay racing, why
don't we ask her to scheme up a relay race for our school
buses?"

Bonnie and the gorgeous Ginny cackled and maybe
Esther and Susan did too. Personally I didn't laugh because I don't see much that's funny about the joke and
even less that's funny about letting down the Pennies
along with every other female in Randolph County. So
that's why I didn't laugh.

It was beginning to feel like a trip without end, when
Mr. Barnes finally brought the bus to one of his precision
stops. Philip and my stop is just where the dirt road leading to both the Lambert Farm and the Hall Dairy Farm
meets up with the highway. " 'Bye," I called to the Pennies
as I followed Philip Hall out the door, but I guess they
were still too mad to talk. Leastways nobody returned my
good-bye.

As I jumped the drainage ditch, now swollen with
swiftly running rainwater, I heard my name called.

"What do you want, Philip Hall?" I asked from my
side of the ditch.

He took a flying leap to join me. "To tell you something."

"What kind of a something?" I asked, guessing by his
strange look that we were going to have a conversation
different from any we had ever had before.

"Well," he said, examining the worn-to-a-point rubber
eraser on his red mechanical pencil. "Before I say a thing,

you've got to promise on a stack of Bibles that you won't tell another living, breathing soul what I'm going to tell you."

"You know I won't."

"On a stack of Bibles and on your grandmother's grave? Promise?"

"Oh, you know you can trust me, Philip, even if my grandma ain't dead. She just lives over the county line in Walnut Ridge."

He took a step closer. "Just 'cause I tell you something for your own good don't mean that I'm a tattler!" he said in a voice so full of emotion that I wanted to reassure him.

"Telling something to help out a friend ain't tattling," I explained, thinking how confusing things sometimes get. I mean, Tiger Hunters were supposed to be Pretty Pennies' natural enemies, but, as any fool could plainly see, the bravest Tiger Hunter of them all wasn't one bit my enemy. No, sir, he was my friend. Maybe my only friend!

This time it was me who took a step closer. "So please tell me whatever it is you have to tell me."

"It's about the Pennies," he said. "They're having a meeting tonight."

"But they couldn't be. The Pennies hold their meetings on Friday nights. Today's Monday."

"I know what my ears heard," he told me, sounding as sure as if his head had no room for doubt.

"Philip, don't you know I'm their president? Who would be there to conduct business and appoint the committees and who would make the suggestions and—"

Philip Hall's head bobbed up and down just as though he not only expected the questions but also knew the answers. "Bonnie Blake wants to be president of the Pretty Pennies really bad. Before you got on the bus there was a heap of whispering about you."

I heard myself sighing. "Reckon I ain't too much blaming them for talking bad about me, Philip, 'cause truth is, I let them down. Let them down real bad."

"Nah, you didn't!" he said, kicking the half-frozen ground. "Leastways not so all-fired bad." His index finger shot straight at me as though he was fixing to tell me off. "You think you is the only team to lose a contest to a better team?" Then he answered his own question. "Nah, you ain't the only team."

For the first time since the relay race, I had found something to smile about. "One thing that I appreciates," I told him, "is your friendship, Philip Hall. Really I do."

"Oh, it ain't much of nothing," he said with an embarrassed smile. "But I done told you all I overheard. There's a secret meeting tonight at Bonnie's."

All the high places along the snake-shaped road that led to the Blakes' farm were touched by moonlight, and yet the getting there wasn't easy. Not at all. I stopped within sight of Bonnie Blake's weathered frame house wondering once again if I shouldn't maybe turn around and hightail it back on home.

Maybe it was for times such as these that phrases like "Leave well enough alone" and "What you don't know can't hurt you" were invented.

Alongside the berry bushes that edged the side of the deserted road I sat down and began speaking to the right friendly-looking face of the moon. "Why would the Pennies be secretly meeting without their president?" Problem is that I'm afraid to learn the truth . . . but even more afraid not to.

After a while just sitting there without moving made me feel, for the first time, cold. I stood up, brushed the dust and bits of dried leaves from the seat of my jeans, and told myself that anything is better than not knowing! Isn't it? Yes! No! I don't know. . . .

As I walked closer and closer to the Blakes', I told myself that anyway it was probably something Philip Hall had misunderstood. After all, I was still the founder and president of the Pretty Pennies Girls Club of Poca-hontas, Arkansas. Not to mention being their chief presiding officer. So how could they have a meeting without me?

The aroma of fresh popcorn bounced along on the night breezes. As I approached Bonnie's house I knew I did not want to be seen. Slowly, cautiously, I tiptoed onto the front porch and peeked inside the lighted window. Sitting on the floor in a half circle were Esther, Ginny, and Susan munching popcorn and listening as Bonnie solemnly read from a sheet of lined paper:

"Because Beth Lambert went around bragging to one and all that we girls were going to beat the living daylights out of the boys, folks just believed, naturally enough, that we were going to win. And that sign! If she had asked me, I would have told her not to hang up that dang fool sign! Why, we hadn't even lost the race when the menfolks were pointing to the sign that bragged, 'See the girls beat the boys'!"

"Don't you know it!" said Susan, stuffing a handful of the popcorn into her mouth.

"Well, the sign was bad and the bragging was even worse," continued Bonnie. "But we all know what the worst thing was."

Ginny's gorgeous head went from right to left. "The worst thing was the throwing. If I live to be a hundred, I'll never understand how she could have been dumb enough to throw that banner when everybody knows you've got to hand it."

Bonnie reached down into the skillet for some popcorn. "Why, if Beth had known anything about relay racing," she said, talking with her mouth full, "she would have known full well not to throw what the rules tell you needs hand delivering!"

"If it weren't for her we would have won that race for

sure," said Susan. "And anyway, what are Tiger Hunters going to do with a Ouija board? Boys don't know the first little thing about Ouija boards."

Bonnie vigorously nodded her head in agreement. "Guess we all know what we ought to do for the good of our club. And no matter how much it's going to hurt us and how much it's going to pain us," she said, smiling as though it didn't hurt a bit, "we all know that the thing we got to do is vote the old president out and vote a new president in."

The worst of my fears came rushing in on me with jarring suddenness.

Bonnie giggled nervously. "Course, I sure do want you all to choose whoever you want for your new president, but right naturally enough I'd be right proud if that somebody turned out to be little ole me. Like my ma always says: 'A new broom sweeps clean.' "

As direct as the straightest of lines, I rushed up to the Blakes' front door. My heart struck like a brutal prize-fighter's fist against the internal wall of my chest. With a quick turn of the knob, I pushed the door wide open. Four faces! Four faces, each of them caught and firmly held by surprise.

I looked directly into the frightened eyes of Bonnie Blake. "You ain't got no right doing what you're trying to do," I told her. "Stealing away my presidency. You and your secret meeting. Ain't no Pretty Penny nowhere on this green earth got the right to do that!"

Just then Mrs. Beatrice Blake, in a pink chenille robe, and Mr. Simon Blake poked their heads in from the next room. When Bonnie saw her folks, she breathed in deeply as though taking comfort from their presence. "And you ain't got no right here!" she said. "This ain't your house, Beth. And you ain't even been invited!"

"When you invite Pennies to a meeting, then you invite me too 'cause I'm the head Penny of them all. The president!"

"Well now, that's just a silly little ole technicality, Beth Lambert," Bonnie called out in that terrible sing-song-sassy voice of hers. " 'Cause there ain't no Penny nowhere who wants you as our president!"

Could that really be true? Oh, God, please don't let it be true. I looked at the Pennies' faces to see if I could read what was written there. While their faces didn't exactly look like doors, they did, for some reason, remind me of doors. Doors that are shut tight. Locked. Barred!

"What I did was wrong . . . is wrong," I said, searching for just the right words to publicly explain what I had never before even privately understood. "And nothing can change that. I still don't, not in a million years, understand how I could do something as dumb—as dummy-dumb-dumb!—as throwing the banner."

I looked down at the floor because I was no longer comfortable looking anywhere else. "And about that sign. Guess I have learned that nobody ever ought to go bragging about winning something they ain't already won."

An unpopped kernel of corn cracked so noisily between somebody's teeth that I plumb forgot what I was fixing to say.

Then I remembered. ". . . But I sure do hope that you Pennies can give me another chance, 'cause that's the only way I can make it up to you. I'll work harder than I've ever worked before trying to prove that I'm not so bad after all."

"I'm not so bad after all," Bonnie mocked in a voice as shrill as an unbroken stick of chalk screeching across a blackboard.

I chewed my bottom lip while wondering if there ever comes a time when murder is not exactly murder. "We'll now put it to a vote," I said, trying to sound presidential. "Does the Pretty Pennies Girls Club of Pocahontas, Arkansas, want a new president or are they plumb happy with the old one that they already got?" I sucked in breath before lifting my own right hand. "All those wanting to keep me in office, please raise your right hand."

When nothing happened, when not another single hand was raised to join mine, I told myself that it would be better if I could have the dignity to quietly accept the decision of the Pennies. But in spite of the warning I had just given myself, I heard myself ask, "Reckon you all want yourselves a new president?"

Bonnie brushed by me. "All those Pennies who wants

the sparkling new leadership of Bonnie Blake, please raise up your hands," she yelled out, throwing up her own two arms with such force that it's a plumb miracle they didn't go flying from their sockets.

I watched the gorgeous one raise her arms, followed by Susan and finally, somewhat reluctantly I thought, by Esther. Suddenly Bonnie let out a victorious "YIPPEE!" which was loud enough to be heard halfway up to heaven's doors. Then I surprised myself by shaking her hand and telling her that I hoped she'd be a mighty good president—every bit as good a president as the Pretty Pennies deserved.

Bonnie gave me a strange look just as if she wasn't sure that I was one-hundred-percent sincere. Actually, I didn't for a single moment blame her. I was too busy feeling too many hurtful things to even be sure myself.

But there was no doubt in my own mind about what I said next. "To tell the truth, I was getting a little sick and tired of having to bear all the responsibilities of being president. So it's plenty fine with me that somebody else is finally taking over." Now, *those* words would have easily won me this year's blue ribbon over at the state fair. That is if they gave out prizes for insincerity.

Chapter 5

A new town ...
a new county

From the rise in the field I could see that our house was
lit by moonlight, and I was surprised. Not one bit surprised by the moonlight, but surprised by being almost
home, 'cause it takes a whole heap of steps to walk the
five miles between the Blakes' farm and the Lambert
Farm, and yet I'd been so deep in thought that I don't
hardly remember taking a single one.

It was more than what had happened at Bonnie's
house tonight. Far more. Had to do with my whole life.

And it had to do with wondering how I could go on staying in Pocahontas with my friends treating me meaner than most enemies.

I opened our front door and came into the light and warmth of the living room. Pa just looked up from reading his very favorite magazine in all the world, *Turkey World.* But my mother called right out, "Beth? Beth, is that you, girl?"

"Reckon it is."

"Know what time it is? Want to tell me where you've been 'til nine o'clock in the nighttime?" she asked, while leading me into her cinnamon-scented kitchen.

I sat myself down at the table. "Nowhere special," I answered, while my arms dropped to the table to make a nesting place for my head. Then my eyes closed for a minute or two and I might even have dozed, 'cause I didn't remember anything until I heard my mother's voice again.

"I made you a mug of steaming hot chocolate," she said. "Just the way you like it, with the marshmallow melting in."

Ma handed me a cup and watched as I took small careful sips. "It's good," I told her, enjoying the feeling of heat traveling down to my chest. After some more silence, I told her, "Ma, I've been thinking . . ."

"Thinking?" she repeated, just as though that was the one activity which I did that made her the most nervous.

"Thinking. Yes'm." And when she just stared at me

without doing anything to break the quiet, I spoke again. "About Pocahontas."

That seemed to surprise her. "Pocahontas? Well, why? It's just a place a lot like other places. The sun comes up. The sun comes down. —So exactly what were you thinking about this ole town?"

"I've been thinking that—well, what I've been thinking is that it don't much seem like my hometown anymore."

Ma looked taken aback. "What do you mean sitting there saying that it don't seem like your hometown? Who else's hometown is it if it ain't yours?"

I shook my head so as to tell her that if she was looking to me for answers, she better look elsewhere.

She went on talking. "Ain't this the town whose Main Street you can't hardly walk down without saying howdy with every step? And don't go forgetting that it was from this town that fifteen men pulled themselves from a warm bed on Abner Brady night to go searching for you!"

"What you say is true enough, Ma, but what I'm trying to say is every bit as true too. Something done gone wrong, 'cause I've been losing so much lately that I've plumb forgotten how to win."

I heard the breath whistle through my mother's teeth. "Now you haven't been losing so long or so much, Beth. Just the Abner Brady award and last week's relay race." I took sips of hot chocolate while Ma went on talking.

" 'Cause ain't I never got around to teaching you, girl, that losing an honest race ain't nothing so serious? You ain't done no stealing and you also ain't done no lying, so why don't you just try and rest easy until all the noise and commotion die down?"

"Thing is," I tried to explain, "I've done lost a lot more than a race and Mr. Brady's award. Something else was lost. Something I never expected to lose."

Ma moved her chair closer to mine. "What was it you lost, babe?"

". . . They made her president. Bonnie Blake. She called a secret meeting and the Pennies up and made her their president."

Ma covered my hand with hers. "I is so sorry to hear that, Beth. I know how important the Pretty Pennies have always been to you."

"What they had was a secret meeting, Ma! And they didn't even want me to know. My friends! My friends? Well, I just reckon that they ain't my friends anymore."

"Your Pennies are holding on to their anger longer than need be. You're going to have to give it some more time and just keep on trying."

I shook my head. "Seems like all the noise and commotion you tell me about ain't one bit dying down. 'Cause what they is doing is all the time growing. Growing stronger and stronger. Reckon I done given up trying."

"You give up trying!? My Beth, of all people, give up trying?!"

"Have to. 'Cause I ain't meeting up with nothing but failure."

"Failure?" repeated Ma, making the word sound almost musical. "Why, failure ain't the worst thing that can happen. 'Cause the very worst thing that can happen is to give up trying."

"It's not so much that I want to give up trying," I corrected. "It's that I want to give up trying here. Here in Pocahontas."

"Well, the good Lord ain't seen fit to put us Lamberts down nowhere on God's green earth but right in good ole Pocahontas, U.S.A."

For a while we were both quiet enough to hear each other breathing. Then Ma spoke again. "Awww, Beth, things ain't good for you nowadays, I know that, but the only thing we can do is to keep on hoping and keep on praying and keep on trying."

"There is something I can do, Ma. I thought about it long and hard all during my walk from the Blakes' farm. You're right that I do have to try again, and I will too. But in some other place. A new town . . . in a new county. In a place where nobody has ever heard of Abner Bradys, relay races, or Beth Lambert. That's what I really want! To go to a place where nobody knows the name Beth Lambert."

"What is you talking about, girl? Do you hears what you is saying?"

"Yes, ma'am!"

"Oh, no, Miss Beth, you don't! Otherwise you'd know that this is your home. The only home you is going to have 'til you up and marry and get a home of your own."

"Well, I ain't saying nothing about permanent. I'm saying that for now I don't want to be living in a place where everybody all the time turn up their noses at the mention of my name."

Ma looked horrified. "Folks in Pocahontas don't do that to you."

"Oh, yes, ma'am, they sure enough do! They all the time pestering me and poking me with their ridicule."

Pa came into the kitchen, shaking his head as though trying to shake away something bad. "Ain't nobody nowhere got no right to be picking on my girl!"

Ma shook her head. "Beth is so unhappy, Eugene, that she want to go to a place where nobody knows her, but I already told her that this is her home. The only home that she has."

"Your ma's right. Ain't no place for you to be but this place! Besides," said Pa, "half the fun and laughter in this house is brought in by you, Beth. Who would make up for the laughter if you went away?"

"It wouldn't be for long, Pa, honest. If I could only go to a place where people can look at me—look at Beth

Lambert and see something excepting my old mistakes . . . well, if I could do that for a while then I just might stop making so many of them."

"I done heard about folks," said Ma, "who have one house to stay in in the summertime and another house to stay in in the wintertime. But, Beth babe, that ain't you. That's them and we is we. Truth is, this is your home. The only home you've got."

"Reckon I know that too, Ma, but I also know I've got to leave it for a while." I thought about the recent days of silent treatment that the Pennies had been giving me. "I want to live in a place where my hi's and my good-bye's will be answered back," I told them. "Let me move, please. Just over to Grandma's house in Walnut Ridge."

My mother sighed, and the sigh seemed to come from deep within her. "Your grandma would be tickled pink to have you. I know that 'cause ever since your grandpa died, she's been powerful lonely. One time she told me that sometimes she talks to her radio and sometimes she talks to her chickens and sometimes she just talks."

"Does that mean you'll let me do it?" I asked, looking first at Ma and then at Pa. "Let me go to Grandma's?"

But my parents weren't looking at me. Ma was staring at Pa and Pa was staring at Ma just as though answers could only be found in each other's eyes. "Well, Eugene," said Ma, breaking the silence. "What do you think about this here kettle of fish?"

For moments Pa stood as still as an oak tree on a

windless day, then finally he nodded. "Your ma and I would sure miss you a whole heap. But seems to me like you were born into this world with a fine head for knowing what you want and what you don't want. Course we'll miss you, but I'm betting you'll want to come back home before too long."

As we six Lamberts walked through the arched doors of the Old Rugged Cross Church, all the parishioners turned in their seats to stare just as if they had never in all their born days seen a real live Lambert before.

We moved sideways along the pew until we reached our own every-Sunday-morning seats. "Looks like they all done already heard the news," Ma whispered loud enough to embarrass me.

But it wasn't until just after the service that I began to understand that the little information folks had heard about me and my plans only served to make them hungry for more.

It was the Reverend Ross himself who was the first to come right out and ask what everybody else seemed too shy to ask. "My dear Beth, it sure is with a powerful sense of loss and regret that I heard the news that you are leaving our fold this very day. Leaving your family, going to a new town. You think you're doing the right thing?"

As he gave my forearm a series of little pats, I finally found a few barely adequate words to answer him with. "Well . . . sir . . . yes, sir."

Moving with her usual full-steam-ahead stride, Mrs. Ross came to a stop next to her black-robed husband. She gave me a smile to indicate in advance where her words were going to be directed. "You think you're going to like a new school? Making new friends?"

I answered, "Yes'm." But it was Luther's answer that made me prideful. "My sister can make all the friends she wants, I can tell you that."

The bus-driving Mr. Barnes joined our little cluster. "When you come back, let me know about the bus drivers over there in Walnut Ridge. Let me know if they're as good as the drivers in this town."

"I'll be close enough to school for walking, Mr. Barnes, but they're probably not even half as good as you."

"Know what it is I want to know?" asked the widow Louise Matthews. That was a question I felt silly answering, but how could I ignore a grown-up old lady? So I answered, "No, ma'am." She stared at me long and she stared at me hard. "What it is you're going to do when you get homesick."

I told her that I didn't know, and then I said a quick good-bye before walking out into the field a ways. Running up from behind, Bonnie Blake led the Pretty Pennies making a half circle around me.

More than anything I wanted to slap that smug smirk off Miss Newly-Elected-President's face. In the Bible it says, plain as anything, that hating is wrong. But when somebody comes along to take something that wasn't theirs to take, then what's a person supposed to feel?

Finally, and with the rest of the Pennies looking on, she spoke sassy. "How come you running away, Beth Lambert?"

Was that what I was doing? Running away? Maybe so. Maybe not. But even if I was I didn't plan to publicly admit it. Leastways not to the new president and chief presiding officer of the Pretty Pennies. "I'm not running anywhere," I said.

Suddenly Bonnie jutted her face within striking distance of my right hand. "Are you running off to someplace where they're going to let you be president?"

I waited until Bonnie and the Pennies stopped their taunting laughter before answering. "Bonnie, it should be perfectly plain, even to you, that I'm standing, not running! And anyway, it's real plain to me that I don't want to be president of anything. Not anymore."

And just as soon as I said that, I understood that the words were true. All true, 'cause I'm all through being a leader. What I wanted was to become the best follower any club has ever had! A not-to-be-criticized-because-I'm-only-following-orders follower!

As I turned away from Bonnie and the rest of the Pennies, who huddled as though for protection behind her, I suddenly realized that they didn't know what to do or how to act. That's when I also understood I had no reason to be afraid of them.

Half galloping, but fully smiling, Philip Hall suddenly appeared at my side. Sweet Philip. Together we walked toward the road where the parishioners' cars and trucks waited beneath the Sunday sky. A sky that seemed to be growing heavy with storm clouds.

For a while we walked quietly while I was all the time thinking how much I was going to miss him. Suddenly he spoke through clenched teeth. "I don't know why you're leaving Pocahontas! If those dumb Pennies think Bonnie is going to be a better president than you, then they better think again. 'Cause she ain't got enough leadership ability to lead a cow to the pasture."

"Well . . . it's been a lot my fault too," I told him, and yet having him take my side was a little like having soothing medicine applied to a very sore place.

"The fun things in this town was because of you," he said.

"I'm glad somebody remembers things that are good about me. —Reckon, I'm going to miss you, Philip Hall."

I gave him the quiet that he needed to tell me how much he was going to miss me, but it went on and on unused. Finally, I just up and said, "Well . . . ?"

"Well," he repeated as though he was finally catching on. "Guess . . . I'm going to miss you too." We both walked in silence for a while longer until he suddenly broke out smiling. "Hey! Want to know something?"

"Sure, I always want to know something."

"Want to know what I think? I don't think you're going to go live in Walnut Ridge after all."

Now that was a new thought. "You don't?"

"Shucks, no! Wait until after your Sunday dinner today when your pa takes your suitcase out to the truck and you're just a-standing there trying to say your last good-byes. Know what you're going to do then?"

I knew only that just his words made me feel a tugging, tearing, body-aching sadness. "What am I going to do then?" I asked, trying hard to sound more lightly cheerful than I actually felt. "Change my mind?"

"Right-o!" he said, wildly slapping his hands together to give his words a kind of extra added emphasis.

As Ma began serving her Sunday dinner specialty, roast turkey with cornbread stuffing, Pa's eyes skipped around the dinner table. Beginning with Luther, his firstborn, and then going on down through Fancy Annie, his second-born, me, his third-born, and finally settling on his last-born child.

"Well, now," he said with his eyes fixed directly upon Baby Benjamin. "For some weeks, little man, you've been getting this family all excited 'cause at some moments you look like you is going to surprise us all by saying your first word."

"Seems like his mind is just brimming over with things he wants to say, but his tongue ain't saying a single word of them," said Ma.

Pa laughed. "Baby Benjamin got himself a stubborn streak that came from his mama's side of the family."

Ma threw him a sideways glance. "Why Eugene Lambert, don't you go saying things about the Fordes in front of your own children, not even in jest. Why, there was hardly a Forde born that wasn't known for their patience and sweet temper!"

"Hold on to your tongue, Sweet Mama," said Pa, laughing again. "Well, now, Baby Benjamin, I was thinking that maybe we could persuade you to talk by giving you something real important to say. Ain't nothing more important than asking the Lord's blessing. So, little Ben, you mind your pa, and begin this meal by asking for the Lord's blessing."

As we watched, our little boy seemed as though he was readying himself for the great challenge. His back straightened, his chin rose, his eyes focused directly upon Pa, his mouth opened, and then, wonder of wonders, Baby Benjamin burped. Burped!

We all laughed until our stomachs hurt and then Pa announced that if his youngest wouldn't lead in the praying then maybe his next-to-youngest would oblige.

I looked down upon a table filled with so many of the things I like to eat: turkey, dressing, mustard greens, cornbread, and sweet potatoes with the marshmallows baked right in. It made saying thanks an easy thing to do.

After a while, when everybody's plates had become

empty enough to pretty accurately count the rosebuds in the design, we cleared the table. And then Ma made an announcement: "Seeing as how this is our Beth's last meal with us for a spell, what we're having for dessert is her favorite dessert in all the world."

"Hooray for mincemeat pie!" I said.

Ma's expression changed from surprise to confusion to anger. "Mincemeat pie ain't never been your favorite dessert, girl, so don't go trying to prove that it is!"

Now one thing I never did like was having folks tell me what it is that I like and what it is that I don't like, 'cause who knows that better than me? "Mincemeat pie is my favorite, always has been my favorite and always will be and there ain't nothing in this world going to change that!"

Ma threw her hands on her wide hips like she was fixing to go marching into battle. "Why, Beth Lambert! Ever since you've been knee-high to a grasshopper, marshmallows been your favorite. Hot chocolate with marshmallows, sweet potatoes baked with marshmallows and your favorite dessert is made with marshmallows too. Chopped nuts, pineapples, and marshmallows."

In spite of myself, I smiled at the thought of my second-favorite dessert. "Heavenly hash ain't bad either."

"I got something for you too, Beth," said Fancy Annie, jumping from her chair and dashing toward our bedroom. Within moments she returned, dangling her best shoes—the ones that came all the way from Mexico.

"It's my huaraches," she announced, just as though I was experiencing failing eyesight. "You can have them!"

"You're giving them to me?" I couldn't believe the incredible news that my sister would actually give me the shoes that previously she had only once in a while allowed me to borrow. When she nodded a shy yes, I threw my arms around her.

"Oh, land sakes!" said Annie, who seemed embarrassed by my sudden show of affection. "Ain't no big deal. After all, it's you been giving them most of the wearings."

Once again I thought how downright peculiar my sister is about things like that. I mean when you try to show her that you love her, she'll look away as though she can't bear to see that love.

But just come to Annie with the complaint that she's been scattering her makeup on your side of the dresser or hogging the bathroom. What do you think she'll do then? Why, she'll look you straight in the eye while taking in every one of your complaining words. Don't rightly know what to think except that maybe some folks feel more comfortable with blame than they do with love.

Then Luther cleared his throat in the funny way he does when he has something important to say. "What I have for you," he said, "is something you can't exactly take with you. Not exactly. But I hopes you likes it

98

anyway. My most precious pig, Miss Pig, who's going to win a blue ribbon at the county fair—"

"Who you hopes is going to win a blue ribbon at the county fair," corrected Annie.

"Who I *knows* is going to win a blue ribbon at the county fair!" said Luther, correcting the correction. "Who is not going to be named Miss Pig anymore 'cause from now on she's going to be called something else. From this day on she's going to be called by her new name—Miss Beth!"

My family broke into applause and I began to wonder if there was any family anywhere better than this one. "Sure do appreciate that, Luther," I told him. "Reckon I feel honored beyond the telling. So thanks a heap. And another thing: I think you're right, Luther. I feel it in my bones. Miss Beth, she's going to win the blue ribbon."

While Ma served the heavenly hash we talked a little more and laughed a lot more and then there came along a pause that was different from the other pauses. Maybe it was because somehow we all knew that this time it wasn't going to be filled by giggles, snickers, wisecracks, or anything else that was fun. Guess we all knew the time had come.

Pa stood up. "Well, if you're about ready, I'll take your suitcase out to the truck."

"Reckon so," I answered, standing too.

Fancy Annie looked lost and maybe a little frightened, just as if it was she, and not I, who was the little sister. The one who needed taking care of. I wanted to cheer her up. "Hey, you're going to have a room of your very own," I told her. "Something you've always wanted."

Annie was either cheered by the thought or else she was just pretending to be. I wasn't certain which.

"Well, 'bye, Luther," I said, leaning over to place a light kiss on his cheek. Somehow I thought he was going to quickly turn his head away, but he didn't.

" 'Bye, sis," he answered, calling me by a name he had never called me before. Sis. I think I liked the sound of it. A lot.

While Baby Benjamin examined the bony remains of a turkey leg, I scooped him up from his hand-me-down high chair. "Got one of your sloppy ole kisses for me?" I asked, spinning around with him as though we were dancing. "Come on now, give Beth a good good-bye kiss."

Without actually doing whatever a person is supposed to do to make a real smacking kind of a kiss, the baby did place his lips against my cheek. Then he moved his face back a ways to look at me. If I didn't know better, I'd think that he wanted to see if I looked pleased. And I did.

I slipped him back into his high chair. " 'Bye, 'bye, Baby Benjamin. 'Bye, 'bye."

His arms reached out in my direction as though he

wanted to forever hold me to this spot, and then he opened his mouth to speak, and this time he did speak. And he spoke with all the strength and clarity of a grown-up boy. It was only a single word, but it was his first word. He said, "Beh!"

"He talks!" shouted out Ma as though she was dazzled right out of her mind by his brilliant solo performance. "Our baby done up and said his very first word and he done said it as his going-away present to you!"

"Reckon it's a going-away present, sure enough!" I said, feeling pretty dazzled myself.

My mother wrapped her good strong hugging arms around me and then she reached into the pocket of her apron to pull out a little glass jar that once had held yellow mustard. Only now it was filled to the top with the very shiniest of dimes. "And this here," she told me, "is my little present for you. For the longest time, I knew that I was saving dimes for something. Only I didn't know what that something was. Not until now."

I gave Ma a wraparound squeeze, squeezing her for this reason and for so many others. For all the times I should have appreciated her, thanked her, hugged her but didn't. All those times when I forgot to, neglected to, meant to, but for whatever reason didn't.

What I wanted to do now was to thank her in real words, telling her what was in my heart, but I was afraid. Afraid that I might sound silly. Afraid that my voice might show how close to tears I was. And suddenly I was afraid too that Philip Hall's change-of-mind prophecy might actually come true.

From outside came three short toots from the truck's horn.

Ma looked at me through eyes that seemed to be touched by gloss. "I ain't going to count the weeks until you come home again 'cause I think I already knows that it ain't going to be too many."

"You do? Know that?"

She nodded. "Oh, you'll be back just as soon as you can feel fine and happy again about being Beth Lambert. Now hurry on, girl. Horn's blowing."

"What?"

Ma pointed toward the door. "Your pa's blowing the horn for you."

"Okay!" I called out, while feeling the pain that Philip Hall had predicted that I would. All that pain plus a good bit more.

But just because my friend was right about the pain doesn't mean that he's going to be right about the other half of his prediction. No, Philip Hall, I can't be changing my mind. Not now that I've got so much changing and rearranging on this ole Beth Lambert to do.

I swung open our front door and ran out toward the waiting vehicle. "Coming, Pa!"

Chapter 6

My grandmother's house

As the mournful wail of a passing siren shattered my sleep that night, it struck me full force that starting tonight, I don't live out in the country anymore. Why, on Lambert Farm, the only wail capable of disturbing the night would have to be coming from a lovesick coyote.

I pulled the quilt over my head and thought about what it's going to be like living right here in the middle of things. Here in my grandmother's house along the side of the highway.

Why, I'd get to see the Walnut Ridge All-Volunteer Fire Department whenever it raced by, and the sheriff of Lawrence County gunning his engine as he chases dangerous criminals up and down Highway 67.

And anytime I get the notion, I'll just up and walk right into town to admire all the pretty things in the windows of Ledbelter's Department Store. While I'm in town, I'll remind myself to trot over to the Walnut Ridge Post Office to study their "Most Wanted Criminal" posters. A person can never tell when they might be able to help out the law.

But even before I went to the Post Office, I'd go to the one place I like even better. Straight to the Capital Theater, where I'd stand for a long time in front just to study all those shiny photographs of the movie stars displayed inside glass cases. Most of the time I can tell from those pictures whether or not I'll like the movie.

The light hadn't yet started to creep in under the window shade. I wondered how long 'til morning. How many hours before I walk, for the first time, up those concrete steps and through the massive double doors of the Walnut Ridge Regional School?

Grandma had told me that the school was so big that they not only had a teacher for each and every grade, but they'd got one lady there who did nothing but take care of the books in the library. Imagine that!

As I lifted the top of my newly assigned desk to begin arranging the fresh new books within, I felt a pair of eyes upon me. Gradually I raised my own eyes until I was eyeball to eyeball with a long-faced girl who looked as though somebody had just finished telling her a very funny story. Has she already heard all about me? If she thinks I'm going to stand being ridiculed here in this new town, she's very much wrong!

"Hi, I'm Specs," she said.

I felt relieved. "I'm Beth ... from Pocahontas."

"Really?" asked Specs, as though I had offered up some pretty shocking information.

Even after I said "Yes," she continued to wear the look of mild shock. I began to wonder if maybe she hadn't heard about me after all. "Why does that surprise you so much?"

She scratched her thin cheek. "My mother used to know somebody over there in that town."

"Who was it?" I asked, feeling a little excited just as though I was about to receive something from home.

"I can't think," she said, without noticeably trying.

"Reckon I know just about everybody who ever lived in Pocahontas," I told her. "Is it a man or a woman or somebody our age?"

Specs allowed as how she couldn't remember much of anything. "Except that the person is nice—I remember my mama saying that."

I could see that our conversation wasn't going to do

much to locate the mysterious Pocahontian. "Reckon that description could fit a lot of people in our town." And I thought about some of the people that the description wouldn't fit at all. Them crooked Calvin Cooks, both Junior and Senior; Mr. Cyrus J. Putterham; and Lowell Peters, who wasn't so much a bad person as much as a person that smelled bad. So I'm not counting Lowell Peters.

When the lunch bell rang, I picked up my brown paper bag and, without exactly an invitation, followed Specs along to the lunchroom.

"I guess you don't wear your glasses all the time," I said, curious about what her constantly surprised eyes would look like covered by glass lenses.

"Oh, I don't wear spectacles at all," she answered looking, if possible, even more surprised than usual.

"No?" I felt as though I had walked smack into the middle of an especially confusing conversation. "Specs?" I asked. "Isn't that a nickname?"

She nodded in a quick, assured way that carried with it the impression that her next words were going to dissolve away the confusion in the same way that country sunshine dissolves the fog. "Well, sure it is," she said while continuing to nod. "You see, they only call me Specs because my real name is Margaret Elaine."

Waiting for Specs at a long lunch table was a solemn-looking girl named B.J. who really did wear specs. Thick squares of glass held together by a bridge of silver-colored wires. And another girl named Millie Mae, who more than anybody that I've ever known seemed to have mastered the knack of twirling spaghetti around her fork.

All during the meal, I sat wordlessly at the end of the table hoping that the girls would invite me to join in the talk, but they didn't. Once I leaned over the table to ask if they liked going to this school, but the only reward I received for my friendly efforts was a stingy two-word reply: "It's okay." Then they almost immediately returned to talking among themselves. Only among themselves.

The next day was Tuesday and again I sat at the same lunch table with Specs, B.J., and Millie Mae. During their conversation that was filled with the names of unfamiliar people and places, I once again tried to make a three-way conversation into a four-way one. This time my question was "What do you all do in Walnut Ridge for fun?"

And again the girls answered with just a miserly two words—"Not much"—before quickly returning to each other's company. Only to each other's.

At lunchtime on Wednesday, I was still trying to decide what question to ask the girls when Specs pointed toward me and announced to her friends that this was my third day at the Walnut Ridge Regional School and that I came all the way from Pocahontas.

Millie Mae looked at me as though somebody was trying to put something over on her. "How come somebody who's lived in a place with all the goings-on that

Pocahontas has would want to live in a boring place like this place?"

I thought about all those vehicles on important missions that travel quickly past my grandmother's house. I thought about the store windows of Ledbelter's Department Store, where the Christmas lights were, on this very morning, already being strung. I thought about the separate room inside this very school that is set aside for nothing but books and magazines. And when I thought about all those things, I wondered how anybody in their right mind could call Walnut Ridge boring.

Millie Mae must have caught a look of disbelief on my face, because she went on explaining. "Oh, yeah, I've heard me a few things about your town. Heard that Pocahontas has itself a boys' club called the Pretty Hunters—"

"The Tiger Hunters," I said.

But Millie Mae went on as though she hadn't even heard my correction. "And a girls' club calling itself the Tiger Pennies, and they—"

"That's the Pretty Pennies," I said, wondering what they were all doing right now. Also I wondered about Philip Hall and did he ever think of me. Well, if he didn't, it wouldn't be one bit fair 'cause I was always thinking about him. Thinking about him and my ma, my pa, Baby Benjamin, Fancy Annie, Luther, and yes, even Luther's most precious pig, Miss Beth.

"I think maybe you're right," said Millie, pointing a

sudden index finger at me as though it was she who was giving me the information. "And folks say them clubs have themselves more fun than a barrel full of monkeys with their three-legged racing smack-dab in the center of Main Street. And the mayor didn't even get mad either. Fact is, he gave them all prizes."

Once again I corrected her. "It wasn't a three-legged race, it was a relay race and everybody didn't get prizes. Only the winners!"

"Well, I don't think it's fair," said Millie Mae with real feeling. "Giving a town like Pocahontas all the fun while our town isn't given any."

"Pocahontas doesn't exactly give out fun the way they give out homework assignments," I explained. "Only fun that's in Pocahontas is the fun that folks search out and find for themselves."

"Is that the truth?" asked Specs, while B.J.'s face expressed the same skepticism.

"Sure it is," I continued. " 'Cause Pocahontas has a lot of people who work pretty good together and kind of make things happen."

B.J. looked very thoughtful. The magnification of her glasses made her brown eyes seem enormous. "Correct me if I'm incorrect," she said. "But didn't Pocahontas have a parade too? With clowns and a marching band?"

"One clown. Two bands," I said, looking at the only girl I ever knew who talked like a teacher without actually being a teacher. For somebody as smart as B.J., running a Parade Day or any other kind of a day would be easier than chewing on a wad of gum. "Why, Walnut Ridge could have a special day," I told them all. "If the people in this town want it badly enough."

The girls looked as though I was telling them one tall tale. As tall as the one about the frog who turns into a handsome prince at the touch of a kiss. "No, really, we could do it. Do almost anything we have a mind to do. What would you all like to do?" I asked, but because the girls looked too immobilized by disbelief to come up with a suggestion, I had to make one of my own. "Why, if we want to, we could . . . could throw a Happy New Year's Day Party for this entire town!"

I couldn't tell if I had made them believe me yet. "You'll see," I said encouragingly. "We can do almost anything we really want to do, but first things first. Because the very first thing we have to do is to call a meeting."

Even though it was still on the early side of six o'clock, the November sky had deepened into purple. At Walnut Ridge's only traffic light I turned left, counted three houses down on the right, and then spotted what I was told to look for: "The white house with the front porch light shining."

It was B.J. Faulk herself who opened the door and there were two immediate surprises. The first was that even though I was early, Millie Mae and Specs were earlier still. Guess after waiting for the better part of three weeks for B.J. to call this meeting that she insisted had to be at her house, we were all real anxious.

And the second surprise was the furniture. Sitting as pretty as you please on matching tables on either side of the Faulks' flowered couch were matching lamps. Reckon the word "fancy" was invented for folks like the Faulks.

B.J. served wedges of store-bought apple pie on small china plates and I thought how nobody that I knew in Pocahontas would actually go out and buy an apple pie. Oh, some unfortunate soul who didn't have their own apple trees might be forced to buy apples, but nobody in their right mind would be caught dead spending perfectly good money buying what they could just as easily make.

After we finished eating pie and drinking hot chocolate, everybody began talking about our teacher, Miss Webber, and how unfair she's getting to be. "She'd rather give you a test," observed Specs, "than look at you!"

At seven thirty, exactly one and a half hours after I arrived, a lot of interesting talk was going on about a lot of interesting people, but the meeting hadn't as yet been called to order. In desperation I whispered to B.J., "About when do you plan on getting everybody quiet? Remember, you called this here meeting so that we could plan a big Happy New Year's Day Party for the town. But you can't have a special day until you first get yourself a girls' club to spark things along."

"Silence, everybody," ordered B.J. with raised hands.

"As you perfectly well know, I called this meeting in order to secure a special day on January first for Walnut Ridge. However, before we can have a townwide festival, we must first establish a girls' club to organize, encourage, and monitor such an event."

Never before in all my born days did I hear so much wisdom pouring from one mouth. I stood up, awed beyond the telling, and spoke. "I think that B.J. Faulk ought to be our president."

Probably neither Specs nor Millie Mae understood B.J.'s truly dazzling leadership abilities, because they both came up with the suggestion that I, and not B.J., should be president. Maybe it was just their way of showing welcome to a newcomer. Sure, that was it. What other reason could there be?

Still standing, I tried to explain. "I thanks you all mightily for asking me to be your president, and I would like to be your president too . . . only excepting for one thing. Back in Pocahontas I learned that I ain't much of a leader, so what I want to learn in this new town is how to become a follower. And if it's all right with you all, I'd like to be B.J. Faulk's most faithful follower."

When B.J.'s nomination was put to a vote, both she and I threw up our hands. Then slowly and with what appeared to be a shocking lack of enthusiasm, Specs and Millie Mae raised theirs.

B.J. smiled presidentially. "I deeply appreciate the resounding confidence that you all have invested in me, and I shall diligently attempt with the plans I make for our first of January festivities to justify that confidence. Thank you all. This meeting stands adjourned."

I tugged at her blouse and whispered again into her ear to unadjourn the meeting at once, leastways 'til a proper name for our club was picked. Our new president wisely and responsibly asked for suggestions for a club name. Soon it became clear that the only thing we could agree upon was that a proper girls' club deserved a proper name.

Somebody called out the name "The Walnutters," but somebody else said that it made us sound like a bunch of crazy people. And then somebody else suggested "The Girls' Club," but we all responded to that with sour sounds.

Like a truly democratic leader, B.J. didn't try (like I might have once done) to push her ideas for names down our throats. As a matter of fact, she was so very democratic that she didn't make any suggestions at all. If I had only (I regretfully told myself) been more like her, then I would have been the kind of president the Pretty Pennies deserved . . . but didn't get.

Because it was already eight o'clock (the time I promised Grandma that I'd be home), I couldn't wait any longer for the girls to decide upon a club name. So while Specs and B.J. wrote prospective names on the back of an old envelope, I whispered still another one of my unasked-for, unneeded suggestions into our brilliant new president's ear. Immediately her eyes grew larger and then she delicately used her knuckles to knock for attention. "Since we collectively think of ourselves as something precious . . . precious like pearls . . . I humbly submit that we name our club 'The Irritated Oysters.' Behold the pearl, for it is the fruit of the irritated oyster!"

And for that suggestion B.J. received (and modestly accepted) applause and even Millie Mae said that maybe our new president had some pretty good ideas, after all. Actually Millie Mae's stingy compliment got me wondering why the others can't see that B.J. is soon going to become a fine leader. Oh, maybe B.J. doesn't know all the ropes there is to know about leading, but that's only 'cause she lacks experience. Why, she's so smart she'll soon learn everything in no time flat.

As I walked along the gravelly shoulder of Highway 67 toward Grandma's, the lights from passing vehicles illuminated my way. I felt a heavy burning ball of anger right in the middle of my stomach. I only knew that I wanted to be somebody else so that I could scream angry words at me!

Who did I think I was? Suggesting this and suggesting that! Whispering this and whispering that! Shouldn't it, at long last, be perfectly and painfully plain, even to me, that B.J. Faulk and the rest of the girls are way too smart to need any old ideas of mine? And anyway, where was my promise? The one I made to myself to be nothing more than an obedient, faithful follower? Leaving all the ideas, advice, thoughts, and yes, whispers too for others to give?

Because haven't I already spent too much of my life being bossy? Trying to use my ideas to become the number-one best leader? And wasn't that what got me into trouble in the first place? So much trouble that I had to leave home?

The table light was on in Grandmother's house, and when I entered the front room, she looked up from her quilting. "How was your meeting, child?"

I slumped down in the ladder-back chair next to Grandma's rocker. "Reckon I'm too dumb to learn much of anything, 'cause I'm still trying to do what I did in Pocahontas, still trying to make things happen. But in B.J. Faulk we got us a leader who's smart. Euuuuu-Whheee! So smart that she won't be needing no leadership help from the likes of me."

With my fist, I struck my thigh. "So if I live to be a hundred, Grandma, I don't think I'll understand why it was me tonight that kept butting in. Always having to give my two cents worth!"

Grandma's chuckle was so low that it needed somebody with my own good hearing to hear it. "Are you laughing at me, Grandmother?"

"Maybe I am. Reckon now you'll want me to tell you why."

"Reckon I do."

"I'll tell you. Since you got yourself an eye for observing things, I reckon you've already noticed that only little children and old ladies are allowed to say what's on their minds without bothering to pretty up their thoughts. Well, since I'm getting to be an old lady, I'm going to tell you exactly what's pressing on my mind."

"Yes, ma'am, guess you can," I said, without having a single idea about what to expect.

"You is giving yourself a hard time, Beth, and I don't like it. I don't like anybody, not even you, giving my favorite grandchild a hard time."

"I don't understand why you say that, Grandma! Just think about all those terrible failures that I had back in Pocahontas and then see if you can still say that!"

She stared straight at me, looking for all the world as though she could see not only through words but through walls. "I is saying it still, child. You is being mighty hard on yourself. You deserve better treatment. Yes, you do!"

The next day I had to practically bite my tongue off to keep from pestering B.J. to tell us how her plans were progressing for Walnut Ridge's big day. And five days after that my tongue was kind of raw from multiple bite marks, but I had to congratulate myself because never, not even once, did I try to worm information out of her. When she was ready to report on her progress, she would. I was sure about that.

Even Grandma agreed, saying, "Now, there ain't no need to worry none about Walnut Ridge's Happy New Year's Day Party 'cause this town got us one person who knows how to make things happen."

But by the second week in December, all of Walnut Ridge knew about the party that was coming. Funny thing was, nobody seemed to be doing any work to make it happen. I became worried. I told myself that I had to think up a tactful way to ask some questions of that amazing brain by the name of B.J. Faulk.

At our own Irritated Oysters lunch table, our new president sat unwrapping a crustless sandwich that she identified as "Tuna fish seasoned with dill—my favorite!"

"B.J.," I began, feeling at the same time both awkward and dumb, for I had no sooner spoken her name than I regretted speaking at all. Why, B.J. Faulk probably knows exactly what she's doing, so who am I to question that girl? If it hadn't been for the fact that her vastly magnified eyes were already staring directly at me, I wouldn't have said another word. Not for the world!

". . . It's about the New Year's Day Party," I said, licking my lips, which had grown inexplicably dry. "The one that we . . . we Irritated Oysters are giving for the entire town."

"Oh, that," she said before taking a dainty bite from the right-hand corner of her sandwich.

It was clear that I had gone too far to go anywhere else but forward.

"Well, you know . . . I know you know that it's already been fifteen days since that meeting at your house, and, well, you haven't told us about all the plans you've made for the party."

B.J. took another bite of approximately equal size from the opposite corner of her sandwich. "Plans?" she repeated, just as if the word were so unusual that she was totally ignorant of its meaning.

"Plans for the party. For the Happy New Year's Day Party!"

"Oh, that!" said B.J. "Well, you see, I haven't exactly had a chance to work on them yet."

At first I didn't think my ears had heard right and then I thought that maybe they had. ". . . Not worked on them?"

B.J. clicked her tongue as though she were being forced to discuss a subject which held very little interest for her. "I've had this book report, you know, to do for English," she said. "And do you have any idea how dreadfully difficult it is to report on a book you haven't read?!"

I told her that I hadn't.

"Well, it is absolutely agonizing," she said in a voice that was becoming more and more whiny in a sympathy-seeking way. "Ever since my mother acquired a winter

cold, I've had housework to do! Making my own bed . . .
picking up my own—"

"We have time," I said, while closely examining the
faces of The Irritated Oysters. "We have exactly twenty-
two days until New Year's Day, and we're going to
need every one of those days to accomplish our goal. But
the first thing that I've got to know is how much you all
want a party?"

"A lot!" said Millie Mae.

"A whole lot," said Specs.

I looked at our president. "What about you, B.J.?
You want one too?"

Thoughtfully she examined the remains of her delicately eaten tuna-fish sandwich before raising her head
level with mine. "Well, certainly, I want The Irritated
Oysters to give a party for our town, who wouldn't? But
it's terribly complicated, you know. I mean I don't know
how to plan a party for two thousand people. Who in
their right mind," she said plaintively, "could possibly
plan a party for that many people?"

Did I hear the answer to B.J.'s question echoing ever
so softly through the channels of my brain? So softly I
could barely hear it? . . . Yes, YES. It was there and now
I knew. As sure as I knew my mother's face, I knew the
answer to her question. "Me," I answered, firmly but
quietly. "Me. I could do it."

Chapter 7

Christmas Day in the morning

On Christmas morning, I woke surprised to find that there was no snow and that the few frail clouds that floated across Walnut Ridge's pastel sky didn't look substantial enough to hold snow. Only once before, when I was seven, did I ever see snow, so I don't know why it should surprise me that we weren't having any now.

But even without the snow, I was having trouble believing, truly believing, that one person, on one day, could have so many things to be happy about. Presents to give and presents to receive, and before noon on this very day all the Lamberts were going to come a-visiting.

I could picture my pa tooting the truck's horn as everybody comes rushing from the house dressed up all Sunday fine. And not less than a moment after the last Lambert climbs aboard, he'll have his truck traveling toward the highway that will take them here.

When I entered the good-smelling kitchen, Grandma was already preparing the annual feast. "I reckon," she said without turning around, "that you is one soul who tears into your presents the first thing on a Christmas morning."

I wondered if my grandmother might not be talking about herself. My own mother tells how Grandma always loved sniffing around her presents. Many days before Christmas, she could be found examining, shaking, and in every way possible trying to determine from the outside exactly what could be found inside. "You want to wait until everybody arrives?" I asked, thinking that she sure must have changed in recent times.

"You can't wait that long," she said flatly.

Now one thing I never did like was having folks tell me what it is I'm capable of doing and what it is I ain't. "Sure I can wait," I told her. "Not only can I wait until after they come, I can wait 'til after they leave."

"Oh, no you can't," she said, sounding more like a little girl than any little girl I could off-the-top-of-my-head think of. " 'Cause I want to open my presents now!"

Barefooted, I raced back into the little room that I share with no living soul to bring from beneath my bed two white-tissue-paper-and-red-bow-wrapped objects. Carefully I adjusted the slightly ailing bow of one slender package before presenting it to her. "This is not something you can use now . . . now in December," I told her, feeling for the first time how inappropriate my present was in this season. Actually I was beginning to be afraid it might be just as inappropriate in any season.

With a strength that nobody could have reasonably predicted, Grandma began ripping through paper and ribbon.

"You can take it back to Ledbelter's," I said apologetically. "Get them to exchange it for something you really do like." But she was so involved in the excitement that she paid me no more mind than Lowell Peters would pay on finding a speck more dirt pressed beneath his already thick-with-grease-grit-and-grime fingernails.

Then just before throwing off the box lid, she stopped short. A second or two passed before she reached with leisurely dignity to remove the cover. "A fan! And I declare, if that ain't the fanciest fan that I ever did see!"

"Comes all the way from Japan," I added with a touch of pride.

Gracefully she opened the accordion-style silk fan and began examining in detail the likeness there of a kimono-clad lady busily fanning herself. Then my grandmother walked grandly over to the mirror to admire herself and her fan.

"You really do like it, don't you?"

Grandma nodded. "Come June when our tin-roofed old church gets so steamy inside that the deacons come around offering those no-account paper fans advertising old man Thadeus Hopkins's Funeral Home, I am going to say, 'No, but thank you kindly.' And that's when I'm going to show off my very own fan, saying, 'This comes all the way from Japan. A Christmas present from my favorite grandchild. My granddaughter Beth.'"

Her liking the fan gave me confidence enough to show her the second gift. "There's something else too," I said, handing her the present, which I had placed inside a paper box that once held tissues.

As Grandma raced with her usual high-energy speed through the outer wrappings, I explained. "I know that ever since you've been a girl you've been wanting to see the ocean, but you ain't never yet got to see it. Someday I'm going to take you to it, Grandma," I told her, but she didn't seem to be paying particular attention. Maybe she just thought I was speaking chatter, but I wasn't. 'Cause what I was speaking was a promise.

Grandma threw aside a crushed sheet of white tissue paper and held aloft a pink-and-sand-colored seashell about the size of a cabbage.

"But 'til we get to the ocean," I continued, "I bought you that shell. Put it to your ear and listen, and from now on anytime you want to, you can hear that ole ocean's roar."

She pressed the shell against her ear, closed her eyes, and allowed the most beautiful smile ever to float gently across her lips. Then suddenly Grandmother left her vision of what might have been sun, baked sand, and mild ocean breezes. "What a selfish old lady I am!" she exclaimed. "Here I am just enjoying my ocean, forgetting everything. Forgetting even to give my Beth her Christmas."

Funny thing was that my grandmother had bought two presents for me too: a year's subscription to *Life* magazine and a foot-high globe that spun rapidly on its axis every time I gave it a twirl.

She laughed with real excitement as I pointed to all the places that I'm going to someday visit: Little Rock and Paris and Detroit. "Knew you'd like your gift, child, 'cause you more than anybody I know was born being nosy about this ole world."

At eleven o'clock Grandma took the baked ham from the oven, and a few minutes later she removed the lattice-crusted apple pie. "They're not here yet," I said, as I decorated the table with red berries and sprigs of holly.

"They'll be along shortly."

"Are you sure?"

"They'll be along," she repeated without looking up from the cast-iron pot she was stirring.

Silently I watched as she stirred, tasted, seasoned, and

then stirred some more. Outside I heard a vehicle crunch gravel as it moved off the smooth blacktop and onto the rocky shoulder of the road. I ran to the window, fully expecting to be disappointed, but I wasn't. "They're here," I shouted. "The folks are HERE!"

As I turned the doorknob, Grandma called, "Don't you go running out without your coat. Want to catch your death from a cold?"

I pretended not to have heard as I rushed bare-armed into the Christmas Day cold. I had been waiting for this too long to wait any longer.

"Hey! Little girl!" Pa yelled, swinging me around like he used to love to do back in the days when I really was a little girl. At the end of our twirl, Ma was waiting to bring me inside her embrace. After that I got me another hug from Anne, Baby Benjamin, and finally from none other than Luther Lambert himself.

I wondered at the amount of teasing my poor brother would have to endure if the word ever got back to some of the guys that he was seen publicly hugging his sister. Why, I bet they wouldn't stop bothering him for at least a month of Sundays.

As Ma hung up her coat in Grandma's closet, I began asking her some of the questions that I had been wanting answers to for so long. "Do you ever see any of my old friends? How is Philip Hall? Have you seen him lately?"

"Oh, I see him from time to time. Saw him Saturday in Pocahontas, but he didn't have no more than a nod to say to me. Later in the day I saw Mrs. Hall and she said that that boy ain't had much laughter in him of late. Nobody seems to know why. But I told Mrs. Hall that he might be suffering from the sudden change in the temperature. Cold weather can sometimes make a person feel right poorly."

I wondered if it could possibly be that Philip Hall was missing me. But no, no, how could that be? How could he miss me when he had the gorgeous Ginny to gaze upon?

Suddenly Grandma's voice called out, "I know you all! I know that there ain't a single one of you that can ever rest easy 'til you find out what Santa done brought."

My mother had her mouth set in that funny way she sometimes does when it's important to keep from laughing out loud. "Well, what do you reckon we ought to do about the problem?" she asked.

"Ain't nothing we can do about it," said Grandma with real feeling, "excepting to let all you can't-wait folks open your gifts right now."

A cheer went up.

"But . . . but," insisted Grandma, still holding up her hands for attention, "next Christmas no matter how much you all beg and how much you all plead, we is going to act more like ladies and gentlemen. We is going to eat first and open later."

"The Christmas present I is praying for ain't going to come wrapped up in no package," Ma said as her arm dropped softly around my shoulder. Inside, Grandma had already begun passing out the gifts.

I knew exactly what she was talking about. Guess I had been expecting her to ask the question: "When? When is you coming home, babe?" Funny thing was that I wanted to come home too. Right now, I wanted to come home so bad that my heart began to ache like a tooth in need of pulling.

Still holding on to four pairs of Christmas socks (three for working in and one for dress-up Sunday) Pa moved to Ma's side. Before speaking, he swallowed. "Did you ask Beth the question?"

Ma looked down at the floor before slowly shaking her head no.

Pa swallowed again. "Well, you already done been here at Grandma's for might' near two months, and—"

"Seven weeks, Pa. Seven weeks yesterday."

"Seven weeks yesterday. That's a long time, girl!" he said with unexpected emotion. "Fifty days is a good hunk of time in anybody's life and don't you go forgetting it!"

"No, sir," I told him. "No, sir, I surely won't."

For moments Pa seemed to be silently examining the construction of his new socks. "What I've been trying to tell you is that your leaving done gone and left a big hole in this family. It sure enough did. So when are you comin' home, Beth?"

"I can't come home again, Pa . . . leastways not yet."

Just then Grandma waved two festively wrapped

packages at us from across the room. "For folks who couldn't hardly wait to open your presents, you are sure taking your own sweet time."

"Listen," I said, looking first at Pa and then at Ma. "Come back to Walnut Ridge a week from today. On New Year's Day we can talk some more. That's the day that the girls' club that I wrote you about—The Irritated Oysters—are having a townwide party."

A worried look crossed my mother's face.

"But . . . but you love parties," I reminded her.

"That's the truth," she agreed. "But just the same I'm right fearful that you'll come away from this like you came away from all those things. Hurting bad."

All of a sudden Grandma broke into our circle to shove one present into my mother's hand and another present in my papa's. "Is you is or is you ain't going to open up your Christmas?"

"Oh, we is," said Mama, beginning to smile. "We most surely is."

Then Ma and Pa began distributing presents as though they were making up for lost time. They gave me a spring-green sweater and an earth-brown skirt that was so pretty and nice and new that I knew it would be a good long while before I would allow myself to wear it on an ordinary, everyday schoolday.

Then it was my turn. I could tell that Pa liked the present I gave him. Three cigars sealed in their individual glass containers. "Why, these are a heap better cigars than Mr. J. Donald Morrison smokes!" he exclaimed.

I told him what I knew to be true. "Mr. Morrison ain't nothing but some old pinch-mouthed rich man, but you, Pa ... you is something special."

"Dancing 'til Dawn," said Mama, squinting to read the label on the small bottle of perfume that was her present from me. "I ain't never in my life danced through the night and I don't reckon that I ever will, but I dearly loves to smell the sweet scent of perfume, so thank you, babe."

It sure felt good knowing that the presents I had chosen and paid out good money to buy was liked so much. But now, as I went to get the three presents that had cost me exactly nothing, I was worried that these would not be liked at all.

As I reached down under my bed to pull out the three packages that were nicely wrapped (even if I do say so) with the brightly colored pages of last Sunday's comics, I saw that Luther and Fancy Annie had followed me. They both held on to a single small box and I understood at once that it was their combined present to me. Probably a present that they had spent good money buying.

I took the gift that they extended to me without giving over my presents to them. "What I wanted to do," I explained, "was to give each of you what it was you wanted more than anything else in this here world. I wouldn't have cared one little bit how much it would have cost me either. Only thing that was important was to give you both what you wanted. But the thing was that after I finished spending for gifts for Grandma, Ma, and Pa, I didn't have enough money left over for nothing . . . nothing excepting two postage stamps."

Fancy Annie looked as though she was hearing wrong. "You done bought us postage stamps?!"

"No, I had to use them to get you these!" I said, giving both packages little farewell shakes before handing them over.

Luther had his present already unwrapped while Anne was still removing the sticky tape. "Hey!" he said as he read the title on the plain-looking booklet that had come to me free for the asking from the United States Department of Agriculture. *Raising Pigs for Prizes and Profits.* "I want to read this!" he said, already beginning to read it.

Just then Annie's wrapping fluttered to the floor and she held up a glossy photograph of a right toothy-looking gentleman wearing a fringed cowboy shirt. "Hank Battle!" she said, just as if I didn't know. "This here is Hank Battle, the singing cowboy!"

Luther pointed to the lower right-hand corner. "And there's his autograph."

"Why, how did you ever in a million years manage to get that?!" asked Annie with awe in her voice. "This picture of my favorite singer with his name writ on?"

"Oh, it wasn't hardly no trouble at all," I told my sister. "All I did was to write him a letter in care of the Zarko Record Company over there in Nashville, Tennessee. I told him how much all us Lamberts enjoyed his singing and then in the P.S. I came right out and asked him for an autographed picture!"

Because Luther and Annie liked their free-for-the-asking presents so much, I didn't feel worthless anymore. Fact is, I felt pretty good. Good enough to accept their present. I slid my finger beneath the red-green-and-white paper, and before I could say "harmonica" I was looking at one. A shiny silver-colored harmonica.

"Well, thank you both kindly," I said, and it wasn't more than a moment later that I already had it to my mouth, experimenting with one sound and then another. Trying to reproduce on this musical instrument the tunes that I was always hearing inside my head.

Then Baby Benjamin appeared at the doorway of my room pulling a long-bodied toy dog with mechanical legs. "Beh ... Beh ... Beh?"

"Hi, sweetie pie," I said, scooping him up. "Hey, I like your pet. Who gave you the doggy?"

"Beh ... Beh ... Beh!"

"No, I didn't give it to you, but I do have something right here for you." I noticed that both my brother and sister were watching with surprising interest. Reckon they wanted to know what kind of a free-for-the-asking present I could find for an eleven-month-old baby named Benjamin.

"It's just a little something that I collected instead of sending away for," I explained apologetically to them all. After all, how could my gift possibly compete with a walking dog? "Here, Baby Benjamin," I said while handing him the cloth sack which had once held fifty pounds of flour.

As he put his hand inside, I explained. "It's lots and lots of little pieces of wood. Some round. Some square. Part of them came from the chair factory at the edge of town, but those empty spools came from a lot of ladies' sewing boxes. But you can build things with it, Benjamin Baby. A whole city if you want to!"

The three of us sat semicircle on the linoleum floor and began teaching our baby how to build fire towers, fortresses, and even walled cities from the blocks.

Because of all the miniature construction, I forgot all about my harmonica; Luther forgot about *Raising Pigs for Prizes and Profits*; Fancy Annie forgot about the king of the singing cowboys, and Baby Benjamin even seemed to forget about the wonders of his fancy mechanical dog.

Finally Grandma called us all from the kitchen to come on in to Christmas dinner. Not only the table but the stove, cupboards, and even the windowsills had food resting upon them. There were apple and lemon pies, baked ham, sliced chicken, lima beans, tomato and cucumber salad, hush puppies, fresh country butter, okra, fiddlehead greens, sweet potatoes, and apple cider.

Pa pretended to stagger under the weight of just looking at so much food at one time and in one place. "What army is you expecting to join us, Mother Forde?"

As we sat down to dinner, he spoke with enthusiasm about the new breed of turkeys he was beginning to raise. "Better meat and more of it," he claimed. And Luther sounded like a young man struck by love when he told of "Miss Beth, the prettiest pig in all of Randolph County. The pig that is sure enough going to win the blue ribbon!"

But at the first break in the conversation, I asked if anybody had heard anything about the Pretty Pennies and what kind of things they might be doing.

Both Ma and Pa looked surprised, but it was Ma who done the answering. "You know, stop to think of it, I ain't heard much about the Pennies for a good while. Not since you done left."

"Oh, we see the girls all right," said Pa. "But we ain't heard much of anything about the club."

"That's probably because Bonnie is too good a president to let the Pennies go around making fools out of themselves," I said.

"You reckon that's it?" asked Ma. "Well, what about this here new club you were talking about—The Interested Oysters?"

"Our oysters ain't one bit interested, Ma. What they is is irritated. The Irritated Oysters."

"I thanks you kindly," she said, but the expression that was now moving across her face looked more suspicious than kindly. "What kind of a situation is you leading these Oysters into?"

"Well, there is something that I haven't written about in any of my letters home."

"Now, Beth, you ain't going and getting yourself into any more trouble?"

"Why don't you just let the child tell you?" suggested Grandma.

I stumbled on. "Better start from the beginning. Don't guess I have to tell any of you that for better'n a year, my head was growing fatter and fatter 'cause I got to believing that I was one great leader. Yes, sir, for a while I thought I could do everything except lead the fishes from the waters."

Suddenly Luther interrupted my explaining by laughing loudly. Then with his hand he struck the table. "Lead the fishes from the waters," he repeated. "Now if that don't beat all!"

"But by the time I left Pocahontas," I continued, "I was believing that I didn't have enough leadership even to lead the fishes *into* the waters."

Ma sighed. "You sure enough was feeling poorly. Why, after the Abner Brady, you began acting like you wasn't worth the bullet it would take to shoot you."

"Yes, ma'am," I enthusiastically agreed. "That's just how I felt too . . . until something done come along to change all that."

Elbows on the table, Fancy Annie was leaning toward me. "What was it that came along?" she asked.

"B.J. Faulk."

"Who?" asked both Anne and Luther at more or less the same time.

"B.J. Faulk. A girl my age who lives right here in Walnut Ridge and talks—EUuu WHEE! Talks better than most people sing. And words?! Why B. J. Faulk is acquainted with words that even some dictionaries ain't yet met up with. So, naturally enough, I thought that any girl that smart would be a wonderful president for our new girls' club. Well, truth is, B.J. turned out to have no more leadership ability than a fly upon the wall.

"You see, everybody was expecting our club, The Irritated Oysters, to do what we said we was going to do—throw the townwide Happy New Year's Day Party. But in the end B.J. couldn't plan it and neither could any of the other Oysters. Only I could do it.

"But you can all judge for yourself exactly one week from today on New Year's Day. And if the party turns out good, then I'll know that I have to be what I am. Not just one of those follow-along followers, but a leader . . . natural born."

Grandma stood up from the table. "Reckon I know that. Reckon I've always known that."

"Why, Grandma," I corrected, "for a few weeks there, you were every bit as impressed with B.J.'s leadership as I was. It was you who reminded me that she was the one person in this town who could get the things done that needed doing."

"Oh, no siree, babe," Grandma said. "Never did I tell

you any such thing! I've known B.J. Faulk all her living life and I've known her mother and her grandmother too for all their living lives. What I can tell you is this: Them Faulks, they talk good, but they don't work so good."

I felt more confused than ever. "But I remem—"

"What you remember," she said, interrupting, "was my saying that here in Walnut Ridge we have us one person who can make what's supposed to happen happen. But, child, that person ain't B.J. Never has been B.J. and to my mind never will be B.J."

Was I beginning to understand? ". . . So that person you was talking about . . . I mean the one that could get all those things done that needed doing . . ."

My grandmother raised her eyebrows as though encouraging me to find the courage to ask the question. So I did. "That person you was speaking about? Grandma, was that person me?"

Grandmother jumped up and clapped her hands. "You! You! Nobody but *you*!"

"If you really always knew," I asked, "then why didn't you come right out and tell me what it was that took me all these weeks to figure out myself?"

" 'Cause," she said, smiling as though she was born knowing the answer to my question. "You done come from Pocahontas with all your stuffings knocked plumb out of you. And nobody, child, is going to believe nothing good about themselves 'til they ups and stuffs their own stuffings back in."

Chapter 8

The Happy New Year's Day party

A full hour before the official start of the party, there were more folks wandering about Walnut Ridge's blocked-off-to-traffic Main Street than grains of sugar in some sugar bowls. And it looked to me like still more warmly dressed people were entering Main Street beneath the great hand-printed banner.

HAPPY NEW YEAR'S DAY

to everybody

Good ole |WALNUT RIDGE, ARK|

come to the party on Main Street
at 2 PM

SPONSORED By:

- The Boy Scouts
  (Mivameechee Chapter)
- The First Baptist Church
- The 4-H Club
- The Irritated Oysters
- The Merchant's Association

- Morningside Baptist Church
- The Rotary Club
- WAYNE Whitmore, MAYOR
- WALNUT RIDGE HIGH School
- WALNUT RIDGE WEEKLY
  JOURNAL

FUN + ENTERTAINMENT FOR ALL!

But the folks that I was looking for and hoping for—
my own folks—weren't anywhere to be seen. Now I knew
that they'll be coming along 'cause there ain't anything
that could keep them away, not today. Not unless . . .
"Grandma," I asked as we moved together through the
throng. "You don't suppose Pa's clutch went bad again,
do you?"

138

"Quit your worrying, child. If something went wrong with the truck, your pa would take it into the garage where they'd fix it good as new."

"On New Year's Day? Everything you can think of is closed tighter than a drum on holidays."

A no-nonsense-looking boy wearing a coat over the official blue uniform of a Cub Scout came toward Grandma and me, pulling along a donkey on a frayed rope harness. "They told me that you're Beth," he said.

"Reckon they didn't lie," I answered, but he seemed to be far too serious a fellow to take any notice of such a small joke.

"This here's the donkey for the pin the tail on the donkey game," he announced. "So where do you want the donkey?"

"Well, we're not doing any pinning. What we're doing is chalk-marking. Marking the tail on the donkey. Take her on over to our president and director-in-chief of games, B.J. Faulk."

"Him," said the boy solemnly.

"B.J. ain't no boy," I corrected, surprised that he hadn't ever met up with the talkiest Faulk of them all. " 'Cause them is just some initials that stand for Bette Jean."

The boy gave a couple of tugs on the donkey's rope harness. "You told me to take 'her' over to B.J. Well, this animal ain't no her, 'cause what it is, is a *him*."

"Reckon I forgot to notice," I said, as the boy obediently went off in search of B.J. Faulk.

"Why, I don't think I've never, not in my whole life, played pin the tail on the donkey with a real live animal," said my grandmother.

"Mark the tail on the donkey," I corrected for the second time. "We do it with chalk."

But she didn't seem to be the least little bit interested in a technical correction, for her eyes, her face—just about everything about her—seemed so filled with expectation, so lit up young. And then I understood that it wasn't just the ocean that my grandmother had never before seen. 'Cause something else that she'd never seen was a real, live, townwide Happy New Year's Day Party.

Ain't nothing that could spoil this day. Please, God, don't let anything spoil this day. The sky did look cloudy, but I crossed my fingers that the rain would stay away. Since there wasn't room for all the Lamberts inside the cab of the truck, a freezing rainstorm would keep my folks away, and it would also send folks already here running for the nearest shelter.

I heard my name being called, and when I looked around I saw Millie Mae waving to me from the huge flatbed of a truck we Oysters had decorated to look like a stage.

To the right of the stage was something very beautiful —a graceful pine tree standing tall enough to look down on any man-made structure in Walnut Ridge. Strings of popcorn, silver tinsel, and red-striped candy canes were scattered among the pine needle branches. And circling the branches were more than a hundred colored lights waiting to be turned on.

Before rushing off to see what assistance Millie Mae, our director of the performing arts, needed from me, I asked Grandma to please . . . please keep a sharp lookout for Ma, Pa, and the kids.

Then I tucked my Number 2 yellow pencil behind my ear, placed my clipboard under my arm, and trotted on over to the stage. "What's up, Millie Mae?"

"There's a fight going on!"

Quickly I glanced around without seeing anything that looked even the least little bit violent. "Where?"

Millie Mae pointed toward the back of the stage, where black-robed singers were mingling with the spit-and-polish members of the band. "The Morningstar Baptist Church Choir says they're not going to perform unless they sing 'God Bless America,' and the Walnut Ridge High School Band says they're not going to perform unless they play 'God Bless America,' " she explained.

"Why, that don't make no never mind. Tell the church choir and the band that they can each perform 'God Bless America.' Folks would dearly love hearing that one twice."

"Yeah, well maybe, but it still won't solve the problem, Beth."

"Sure it will."

"No, you see, each group not only says that they got to perform that song, they both insist on opening the program with it."

I scratched my head. This was going to take all the wisdom of Solomon and then some to solve. Again I scratched my head and came up with an idea. "Go and tell each group that what we all want to hear is the glorious voices of the Morningstar Baptist Church Choir singing as that wonderful Walnut Ridge High School Band plays 'God Bless America' for them."

As Millie Mae spoke in conciliatory tones to first one group and then the other, I heard my name being called from another direction. And before even turning around, I already knew it was the voice I had grown up hearing—and loving.

"MA!" I shouted as I leaped off the better-than-chest-high platform. When the force of the impact brought on some moments of pain, I told myself that next time, no matter what, I was going to use patience . . . and the stairs. Barreling through several layers of people, I called her name again, "MA!" just before reaching out and hugging her. "PA!" I shouted, hugging him too. Then Fancy Annie kind of came up behind to give me a shy hug and so too did Luther Lambert.

I took Baby Benjamin, who felt heavier than he had the week before, into my arms. "All I could think about was that because of some old broken clutch you all wouldn't make it to the party," I told them. "And I sure didn't want that to happen, 'cause I've been missing every one of you so bad that it hurts."

"What broken clutch?" asked Pa, looking as though there was something he didn't know but ought to.

"Oh, it was just something imaginary that I was afraid might happen," I tried to explain. " 'Cause I didn't want anything to keep you all from being here with me today at our Happy New Year's Day Party."

Suddenly I felt some little attention-getting pokes to my back and twirled around. And there was Ginny, the prettiest Pretty Penny of them all, looking as though she had found herself the butt of a very embarrassing joke. Directly behind Ginny were Esther and Susan, stretching smiles across their faces. Such silly faces! There was a time not so long ago when I thought they were all right nice-looking faces, but I didn't so much think so anymore. No, not even Ginny's. Something had changed. What had changed?

All three of them said hi and I said hi back, but the words between us seemed stiff. Reminded me of a hinge that had become almost unworkable due to lack of use . . . and care.

"Some folks in Pocahontas got wind that you was putting on this party for Walnut Ridge," said Ginny. "So as many of us as could came on over for the fun."

"Oh, okay," I answered, not really knowing what to say . . . or to feel.

"Bonnie doesn't even know we're here," she said.

"I don't think I like things that are secret, Ginny," I answered her, hoping that she would remember why.

Esther looked me straight in the eye. "Bonnie thinks she's such a good president, but she's not! Know what we've done ever since you've left? We ain't done nothing but eat popcorn and talk."

"That's the gospel truth," said Susan, shaking her head as though she was plumb disgusted. "We don't do nothing anymore that's interesting."

I think I understood why they were telling me all of this, but maybe I needed to hear it from them, in real words that come straight from their mouths. "Well, why are you all telling me this?"

"Well . . ." said Ginny, whose train of thought seemed to have very quickly derailed.

"Well, you see," said Esther as though trying to take up where Ginny had left off, "we is real sorry about what happened. About what we did to you."

"Really?"

"Sure enough," agreed Susan. "And what we want is for you to come back and give us back our fun."

Guess it's nice when friends decide that they would rather have you than not have you. At one time, especially on that night of the secret meeting, I would have given everything I owned (and then some!) just to hear the words that I was hearing now. Only now they didn't seem to be all that important. Not really very important, at all.

"And you can be president and chief presiding officer of the Pretty Pennies, just like before," Ginny was saying.

"Oh, but you've already got yourself a president and chief presiding officer," I reminded them. "And Pennies ought not go changing their presidents in secret meetings, 'cause it hurts that way. It hurts a lot."

All the Pennies looked as though they had plumb run out of things to say. But then, just as if she had a new and happier thought, Esther's face brightened. "Phil's looking for you," she said.

First I searched her face and then the others' for the awful clue that she was fooling me, but I didn't spot it. Not on Esther's face or on Susan's or even Ginny's. "Philip Hall is here?!" I asked. "And looking for me?"

Ginny pointed across the now people-packed street to a solitary figure shinning up a lamppost. "There he is," she said. "Trying to rise high enough to find you."

Without pausing long enough to say 'bye, I zigged and zagged my way through the holiday crowd until I stood directly beneath the dangling feet of Philip Marvin Hall. Jumping up, I gave a welcoming tap to a highly polished brown shoe. His head shot downward and his face showed that he didn't take lightly to being bothered. But that was just for a moment—just until he realized that his botherer was me.

"Beth!" he called, sliding down the pole. "How-DY!"

"Howdy, Philip Hall," I answered, suddenly remembering just how handsome he looks when he smiles.

He spread his arms to indicate the huge gathering. "Boy, you done done it again, girl! This is some fine Happy New Year's Day Party."

"Well, I didn't exactly do everything. I did only the sparkplugging. It was the town that went ahead and did the work."

"There are a heap of folks here from Pocahontas, and all of them are wishing that the party wasn't in this town, but in our town," said Philip, sounding truly amazed. "Mr. and Mrs. Timothy Flood are here, and three of the Pretty Pennies, three of us Tiger Hunters, Sheriff Miller, Miss Eleanor Linwood, Lowell Peters, Mr. Cyrus J. Putterham, Mr. Finn of the tractor company, and I don't know who all. As soon as they heard that you was running the party, they knew it was going to be special."

I don't know how it happened—neither one of us had suggested it—but we were walking away from the people and toward the relative quiet of a side street.

"I'm real glad some Pocahontas people came," I told him. "But if they think that I'm going to make a special fool out of myself"—I said, suddenly shaking a finger at him—"they is going to be mightily disappointed! 'Cause this time I didn't go around bossing everything and everybody!"

"I never said you did," he said, looking a little hurt.

"No," I said, breathing in deeply. "I know you didn't, 'cause you were real nice to me when I won . . . and especially when I didn't. And I reckon I've missed you, Philip Hall."

He smiled a smile that was meant only for me. A show of good teeth and strong jawline. I began to wonder if there wasn't something a little bit magical about that smile. As I watched, it turned softer and seemed to come more from his eyes than from his lips. I thought maybe, hoped maybe, that it was because he was looking at something or somebody he liked: me.

"I understands why you up and left Pocahontas, Beth. And I don't rightly blame you, not a bit. Folks gave me the award that should have gone to you. I know now that I ain't even half the Abner Brady that you are."

"Why, Philip Hall." I heard my voice go soft as sponge cake. "You get on out of here, boy!" I said, while taking his hand so that he couldn't possibly obey. "You did too deserve Mr. Brady's award. Back then I thought you didn't, but now I know you did."

"You know now—for a fact—that I did?" he asked.

I nodded. "You were the best leader and there ain't no doubt about that, 'cause you didn't go getting too big for your britches. It was me that done that. Remember? Remember the old Beth Lambert who was always going around expecting folks to do what she told them 'cause she thought she was such a hotshot leader?"

He kicked a small stone down the street. "Aww,

you weren't all that bad. Fact is, you were a lot of fun." He gave me a couple of taps on the shoulder. "Ain't nobody but you could have given Pocahontas their relay-race day."

"And nobody but me," I added, "could have got so excited that they threw what had to be handed."

"Threw what had to be handed," he repeated, as his warm-throated laughter began to shake his body.

"I don't know why, but I got so excited . . . that I . . . I . . ." My own laughter was interfering with what I was trying to say. Then it struck me—was I really laughing about what I thought I would spend my life crying over?

Reckon it didn't matter none that laughter kept me from finishing my sentence. Philip Hall must have known exactly what I meant to say, because his own body was shaking so hard he couldn't walk. About all he could manage to do was to lean for support against a parked pickup truck.

After a while, when even the most serious attack of the giggles must come to an end, Philip Hall looked at me long and hard. "When are we going to have fun again? When you coming home, Beth?"

Running just behind his question was my answer. But it was one answer that I knew I had to share.

I got a better grip on his hand before leading him into my run. "Come on with me, Philip Hall. My folks been on pins and needles for a mighty long time waiting for me to answer that very question."

We ran until we reached the opposite end of Main Street, where the crowd had thickened into an unmovable mass. "I know we can find my ma and pa," I told him, "because they were right down here in front of the stage."

"Well, how we going to get there? Everybody in town is already pressed in there waiting for the show to start!"

"Like this!" I answered, using my right shoulder to slice both Philip's and my way through layers and layers of people. And there they were. By the stage just where I expected them to be. "Ma! Pa!" I hollered, still holding tight to Philip Hall's hand. "Want to know something? It's time now. Time for me to come back home again."

I watched their expressions of pure shock change gradually into pure pleasure.

Suddenly the multicolored lights of the Happy New Year's Day tree went on as the Walnut Ridge High School Band began playing and the Morningstar Baptist Church Choir began singing "God Bless America."

I felt my heart joining all those other singing hearts asking God to guide the land that we all love. When they got to that part about the mountains and the prairies and the oceans all white with foam, I could see it all shining and beautiful. There in the picture show of my mind.

Philip and I stood so close together that it was his

voice above all the others that I heard singing. Standing on my tiptoes I spoke directly into his ear. "The words that are going to be sung next, Philip Hall," I told him, "them is the best words of all."

"God bless A-mer-i-ca,
My home sweet home."

Bette Greene

grew up in a small Arkansas town and in Memphis, Tennessee. She is the author of *Summer of My German Soldier,* an ALA Notable Book, a National Book Award finalist, and a 1973 *New York Times* Outstanding Book of the Year; *Philip Hall likes me. I reckon maybe.,* a 1975 Newbery Honor Book and a 1974 *New York Times* Outstanding Book of the Year; and *Morning Is a Long Time Coming.*

Mrs. Greene now lives in Brookline, Massachusetts, with her husband and two children.